trick *of the* mind

Other books by Judy Waite

Shopaholic

trick *of the* mind

J U D Y W A I T E

atheneum books for young readers
new york   london   toronto   sydney

Atheneum Books for Young Readers
An imprint of Simon & Schuster
Children's Publishing Division
1230 Avenue of the Americas
New York, New York 10020

First published in England in 2003 by Oxford University Press

Book design by Ann Zeak
The text of this book is set in Mrs. Eaves, DIN, Aldine, Garamond 3, and Frederic.
Manufactured in the United States of America

First U.S. Edition, 2005
10 9 8 7 6 5 4 3 2 1

Library of Congress Cataloging-in-Publication Data
Waite, Judy.
Trick of the mind / Judy Waite.—1st ed.
p.   cm.
Summary: The struggles of several young people who confront family problems, emotional problems, unrequited love, mystery, and violence, is told from the viewpoint of Matt, who is known for his unusual behavior but who also has unusual gifts, and Erin, who tries to use her proficiency with magic to attract Matt.
ISBN 0-689-87014-0
[1. Magic—Fiction. 2. Family problems—Fiction. 3. Interpersonal relations—Fiction. 4. Emotional problems—Fiction. 5. Miracles—Fiction.] I. Title.
PZ7.W13325Tr 2005
[Fic]—dc22   2003063749

For Rachel

Acknowledgments

With sincere thanks to magicians
Derren Brown and Duncan Trillo
for sharing both their knowledge and time

I never dreamed I'd hurt Matt, but everything got so muddled. It was like not being able to tell the difference between clubs and spades. Diamonds and hearts. Right and wrong. Truth and lies.

And it's been so hard trying to get those pictures out of my head. Pictures of him and her together. While that dark splay of hair still keeps rising and rising. I know it will haunt me forever.

I can't put the clock back. I can't undo the terrible thing that I did. But at least I've been honest. And once Matt understands what made everything get so tangled up and twisted, I'm sure we can start again. We'll go back to the beginning. Only this time it won't be him and her—it'll be him and me. Together.

I've never had a girlfriend. I don't reckon I ever will now. It gets me down sometimes, to tell you the truth. On the bad days.

I'm okay-looking. Not great, but okay if you

go for tall and a bit gangly. But even before everything got screwed up I had this image stuck to me from schooldays that I couldn't shake off. I can trace it all the way back down to infant school. I was the sort of kid who was in trouble a lot. I didn't mean to get in trouble, but I got these voices in my head. I never knew what they said—it was like they were murmuring behind a closed door—but they stopped me from concentrating, and I couldn't get my work done. I never told anyone about the voices. I'm stupid, but I'm not stupid, if you get what I mean.

I got in trouble for other stuff too. I used to sit next to Billy Owen. One day he brought this moth to school in a matchbox. I could hear it bashing itself against the sides all morning and it did my head in, just knowing it was there. So at lunchtime I nicked the box from Billy's drawer and hid round the corner in the boys' loo. The moth didn't move or anything and I reckoned I was too late so I held it in my hand, just whispering that I was sorry even though I knew it couldn't hear. It had these velvet brown wings with splodges and patterns and it hit me that I'd never looked at a moth that closely before.

Only then my head went sort of fuzzy, like everything was a long way away, and my hands felt as if they were burning up. Somewhere in the background the voices were going on at me and I got the idea they were excited—sort of jostling about and trying to push to the front, if you get what I mean. And then Billy appeared. He laughed and said I was weird because I'd been swaying, and he tried to snatch the moth. I yelled at him to get stuffed and all the shouting brought Mrs. Dolan storming in. Billy told her I'd been trying to pull the moth's wings off, and he was trying to save it. It really got to me, him saying that, because I wouldn't hurt a fly.

The moth turned out to be okay. It suddenly fluttered off to the ceiling in the middle of all the fuss, but Mrs. Dolan refused to listen to my side of things. She made me stand in the corner of the classroom with my face to the wall. After school my mum got called in. It caused a stack of trouble; but to tell you the truth, I was always getting stuck in corners for something—especially things to do with Billy.

I got good at staring at walls.

So even when I hit my teens everyone in Leigh Cove still remembered me as this geeky kid standing in corners and I guess it didn't make me a great catch. I always thought if girls would give me a chance and talk to me properly I'd be witty and amazing and they could get a different idea about me. In my dreams! It didn't stop me wanting girls though. I used to hang around places where I thought they might show up. The castle was my favourite. Loads of girls went there. Some of them did drugs and stuff, but I never touched anything like that. I couldn't see the point.

But whether they were high or not, the girls at the castle didn't take much notice of me. They noticed Billy though. He'd turned into the sort that girls go for. He looked pretty good and he was a bit of a joker, too. He did stuff to get a laugh. But he could switch moods just as fast as you can click your fingers. Not everyone knew that about him. It was Billy, of course, who was going out with Kirsty. That should have been enough to make me keep away from her. But it wasn't. And I didn't. And that's why everything's got screwed up the way it has. I should have just left her alone.

I first met Matt up at the castle. Everyone calls it "the castle" but it's really a ruin— crumbled grey stone and skeletal towers rising up from the top of a hill. You cross a rickety bridge to get into it, and the moat is all choked with cans and condoms and clutter like that. Someone's even dumped a Tesco's trolley in there.

There's still a portion of castle roof by the east wall and on that day I was sheltering under it doing magic tricks. I'd never been to the castle before, but I'd spent ages watching it from my bedroom window and imagining the wind whispering in the tower while the sea smashed about below. I love things like that.

The problem was that the Leigh Comp. gang went up there. The really rough ones. I needed a back-up in case they turned on me.

The magic tricks were my answer. They always have been. I went up to the castle early, racing there as soon as school finished at half past two. I wanted to get some things sorted before anyone else arrived. It's part of what magicians have to do—always thinking and planning ahead.

I didn't get long enough to soak up the scenery, but it was long enough to get the magic sorted. I was already flicking and shuffling cards by the time the gang came jostling in through the archway.

Matt was with them. Kirsty Carter was there

too. She was with Billy Owen and they were all over each other. Then out of the blue Billy said to me, "Go on then, impress us."

I was surprised. I hadn't expected him to even notice me. But I rose to meet the moment.

"Pick a card. Any one you want. You can show everyone else, but don't show me."

Billy took a card and started spinning it in the air. I could see he just wanted the attention—he was that sort—but the gang started clapping and cheering. I had to block it all so I could keep concentrating.

"Now write your name on the card."

I noticed Billy had horrible stubby fingers. I notice hands. Magicians have to look after their hands, especially if they're doing close-up work.

Billy took my pen, wrote something, and then waved the card at the others. It was obvious that he hadn't written his name. I made a pretty good guess at what he *had* written though. I blocked it out again, and kept going.

"If you put the card back in the middle of the deck I'll show you something."

"There's not much you've got that I'd want to see."

Even I couldn't put a block on that. Everyone creased up and I wished there was a secret trapdoor in the ground that would open up and let me disappear; but I don't do those sorts of illusions. I turned the top card over, ignoring his stupid scrawl, and showed it to him. "Is this it?"

Usually I take a bit longer with that trick and make it the second card I turn over—pretend I've made a mistake the first time so that I can build up tension—but I didn't want to prolong the agony with Billy. I just wanted him to go away.

He actually looked confused for a moment. "I don't get how you did that."

I think it might have bothered him that I'd actually got it right, because not long after that he grabbed Kirsty and they disappeared round the back of the castle somewhere. I didn't suppose he'd stay bothered for long, but I was more knotted up than an Indian rope trick inside. I felt exposed and humiliated in front of Kirsty. Billy was older than me—in the sixth form—but Kirsty was in my year and she looked like one of those models on the front cover of *Gossip*. In my fantasy dream world I wanted to hang round with her one day, and I hated the idea that she'd think I was a geek.

It was back in November—a Friday afternoon—the day I first picked Kirsty out. I was up at the castle, sort of hanging around on the edge of the Leigh Comp. gang.

Billy had Kirsty wrapped round him. In between sticking their tongues down each other's throats they were watching a kid shuffle cards by the east wall.

I remembered Kirsty from school. She'd been this kid with really long plaits who was a couple of years younger than me. I didn't know much about her, but sometimes her mum had these bruises on her face. I never saw her dad.

On that Friday I noticed how much older she looked. Girls do that, don't they? They just suddenly change so that one minute they're someone you don't even nod at in the corridor, and the next minute they've turned into someone you dream about every second of the day and night. I get like that about girls sometimes.

Pox was with me, perched on my shoulder. She lived at the castle. Or, at least, she'd just turned up one day, and stayed. Everyone reckoned she was the ugliest pigeon in the world.

She only had one eye and she was all scabby and scruffy but I really took to her. I often go for stuff that's scabby and scruffy. I used to nick toys from Mum's church jumble sales—bashed-up teddies and rabbits with their ears missing. I hid them under my bed and tried to "wish" them better before I went to sleep. If Mum found them she'd go loopy because she reckoned they were full of germs and she didn't want them "contaminating" the house.

So anyway, I was watching Kirsty do all this snogging and stuff with Billy, and then Billy came up for air and started watching the kid with the cards. When he did that Kirsty looked round at me instead. I could feel her shooting me these short, daring glances, and I was shooting glances back. Every time our eyes met it made my gut go all knotted up like guts do sometimes when you think something really exciting is about to happen, even if it never does. Then Billy caught me looking at her. I slid my eyes away and made out I was only interested in the girl doing card tricks.

In fact, just to make a point of it, I watched really closely. She looked young. Younger than Kirsty anyway. She was wearing a Leigh Comp. uniform but I hadn't seen her before so I guessed she was probably new. Although I didn't know everyone at Leigh Comp. anymore. I left in Year Nine because they reckoned I wasn't coping. I was supposed to go somewhere else but I got a bit panicked about the whole thing and so then they got me a home tutor. Then another one. Then another one. You probably get the idea.

"Pick a card." The girl held the deck out to Billy. "Any one you want. You can show everyone else, but don't show me."

Billy pulled a card from the deck and waved it at the rest of the gang, who all made hooting noises like they were a TV game show audience or something. I felt pretty sorry for the girl.

She looked a bit nervous but she kept going, and gave him this pen. "Now write your name on it."

Billy wrote on the card and then waved it at the gang again. The hooting got louder and I reckoned he'd written something that wasn't his name, although I couldn't see from where I was standing.

"Now I'm going to look away, while you put your card back somewhere in the middle of the deck."

Billy pushed the card back in.

"Okay." The girl looked round again. "Now even though you wrote on that card, and you put

10

it back in the middle yourself, I want to show you something."

The hoots got so wild it was like someone had just won a million quid.

Billy gave this slow smile like he was being witty and amazing and said, "I don't think there's much you've got that I'd want to see."

I reckoned that was a real slimeball thing to say. Not every girl can look like Kirsty Carter.

The magician girl kept her eyes on the cards like Billy hadn't even spoken and slowly turned the top one over. Then she handed it to him. "Is this it?"

Billy's grin froze for a second. "I don't get how you did that."

He waved the card in the air. This time I could see that what he'd written had an *f* and a *k*, and it wasn't hard to work out what went in between.

While he was still grinning round at everyone Kirsty flashed a smile at me that showed off a tiny green emerald on her front tooth. It really got to me, that emerald. I started thinking about where else she might have emeralds. And not just emeralds. I mean—a girl like Kirsty would go for all sorts of body piercing and tattoos and stuff.

She and Billy went soon after that. Billy dragged her away—probably for a session round the back. Billy was always bragging about how he'd had a session with this girl or that. Except he usually called it something else.

Once Billy and Kirsty had disappeared round the back of the castle, the rest drifted away. All except Matt. I noticed him properly then for the first time. I knew most of the others from school, but I didn't recognize him.

He was bone thin and beautiful. Beautiful isn't a word you're supposed to use for blokes, is it? But it was the word that flooded my head when I looked at him. Beautiful. Beautiful. He had a pigeon perched on his shoulder. I thought it showed he must be really special. A bird would have to be careful whose shoulder it sat on.

"Shall I try a trick on you?" I held the deck out to him without waiting for him to answer. "Pick a card. Don't tell me what it is yet." I'm not usually pushy, but I didn't want him to go.

He was wearing a black scarf and he twisted the ends between his hands as if choosing a card was a huge life-changing decision.

"Got one," he said.

I closed the deck up. "Okay. You can tell me now."

"The ten of spades."

I loved his voice. It was soft. So soft. Words like velvet. I was struggling to concentrate, but I shuffled the deck and tried to sound normal.

"That's odd. The ten of spades is missing. Are you sure you put it back in?"

I pretended to look worried, searching up my sleeves and in my pockets as if it might have been hidden somewhere. Then I bent down and made a show of lifting a lump of grey rock. Underneath it was the ten of spades.

"How . . . ?" He was like a little boy, his eyes all lit up and amazed. Magic does that to people. It's one of the things that's so wonderful about it.

I remember he came and stood really close and his hand brushed my arm. It was the lightest touch but it felt electric, like a buzz of lightning. I'd never had a feeling like that—not ever in my life before. I just dissolved. I turned into a complete and utter blob. I hoped he wouldn't notice, but if he

13

did he didn't say anything. He just kept looking at me, and in between the fumbling I kept
looking at him. I'm not good with people. I
worry about whether they like me or not, and
I can never tell what they're really thinking.
But I got a feeling about Matt. It was a huge
sense that he didn't fit in. I knew what that
was like and I was filled with a wild urge, even
then, to get hold of him and hug him. I
wanted to squeeze all of that sadness out.

But it's not the sort of thing you can tell
someone when you've only known them for
ten minutes.

Suddenly, just as I was thinking that
he'd probably be wanting to go off and find
a Kirsty lookalike to break his heart over,
he smiled and said, "You're good. Really
good."

He didn't say anything more than that,
but it was a magic hoop to hang my hopes on.
Maybe, just maybe, he was interested. I went
more blobby than ever.

"I've got better tricks at home," I managed to blurt. "Not just cards, but all sorts."

I thought I could pull myself together
once I was on home ground and show him
tricks that were really wonderful. I know it

sounds as if I was showing off, but I'm confident with magic. It's the one thing in the world I can really do.

"I'd like to see some," he said.

The hoop was spinning. Sparkling. "Come round tomorrow, I'll be in all morning. It's 11 Denton Drive." I dropped a card as I said it, which was a bit embarrassing. I never ever drop cards, unless I do it deliberately as part of my act. Matt picked it up for me and I mumbled my thanks, but I couldn't think what else to say, so I went.

Once Billy and Kirsty had gone, the others started wandering off too.

"Shall I try a trick on you?"

I sort of jolted when the magician girl spoke to me. I'd been staring after Billy and Kirsty and had almost forgotten she was there. I didn't want to be "tried on." Watching Billy and Kirsty go off together had got the voices going again. They were really getting to me and I wanted to break away from everyone and everything and just sit in my room with my music up loud and not answer when Mum called even if I heard.

But the girl had the sort of look about her of someone who wouldn't fit in many places, and I had pictures in my head showing me she was getting a rough time of it at Leigh Comp. I couldn't just walk off, so I put Pox down and turned back to her. "Okay."

She fanned the deck out in front of me. "Pick a card. Don't tell me what it is yet." Then, closing the deck up, she went on, "Okay. You can tell me now."

"The ten of spades."

She shuffled through her deck, then bit her lip. "That's odd. The ten of spades is missing. Are you sure you put it back in?"

"'Course I am." I wondered if she was about to accuse me of nicking it. People get like that with me sometimes. I just think we're getting on okay and suddenly they have a go at me, and half the time I don't even know what it's about. She didn't have a go at me though. She just bent down to this rock that was wedged against the wall and lifted it. It was mossy and had grass growing round it. I reckon it hadn't been moved for a million years. But underneath, face up, was the ten of spades.

"How . . . ?" I went to the rock and checked it all over. My hands got all smeared with mud and I kept shaking my head. The girl was shuffling and flicking the cards about, moving the top one

16

to the bottom without touching it. She looked really intense, like what she was doing actually mattered to her, and I started wondering what it would be like to feel that way about something. Anything at all.

"You're good. Really good."

"I've got better tricks at home." She was shuffling those cards like they were the most important things in the world. "Not just cards, but all sorts."

I don't know why but I felt this rush of sadness for her then, like she was a one-eared bear at a jumble sale or something. It even made me want to cry. I got that a lot—that wanting-to-cry feeling. Not that I ever did. Blokes don't, do they? So instead of crying I said, "I'd like to see some."

"Come round tomorrow. I'll be in all morning. It's 11 Denton Drive." She dropped a card as she spoke, and went sort of flushed in the face.

I picked it up for her. I didn't blame her for going all flustered. I knew Denton Drive—it's the scummy end of Leigh Cove. Grey houses with gardens stuffed full of nettles and weeds and mattresses people can't be bothered to take to the dump. I'd never really thought about it before and I'm not a snob, but I suddenly reckoned it must be rough having to say you lived there.

She took the card off me, gave a sort of half nod, and went.

I saw Billy and Kirsty as I was leaving and Billy started picking on me again. It upset me but I was over the bridge by that time so hopefully Matt didn't see. I didn't want him to feel sorry for me.

As the magician girl crossed the bridge over the moat Billy and Kirsty came back. They were both laughing in that high crazy way people do when they've taken something. Billy jumped sideways and blocked the girl's path as she passed them, making her dodge one way and then the other. "Shall we dance?" said Billy, his face pushed up really close to hers.

"Give her a break." Kirsty gave him a punch in the ribs.

Billy grabbed Kirsty's wrist and started arm-wrestling her, twisting her round and pulling her against the handrail. They were doing that dizzy, high laughing again.

I got this churned-up feeling then, like something bad was going to happen, and I felt so sick I suddenly couldn't watch them any-more, so I watched the girl instead. She was walking really fast, her head high, as if Billy being in her face like that hadn't bothered her at all. But a moment later, as she started hurrying down the hill, she lifted her hand to her cheek. Even from the back view I could tell she was crying.

It got to me, seeing her all cut up like that, so I left the castle and followed her. I couldn't face staying around Billy and Kirsty anyway. I deliberately didn't catch up with the girl though. I just kept behind her all along Station Road, making sure she was okay. A car came up behind her really slowly—a clapped-out red Nissan driven by a bloke with a beard—but she didn't look round. The car did a U-turn and went off the other way, so it wasn't up to anything, but I guess girls always have to be careful.

I stopped following when PC Barlow came cruising past. He parked just level with me and got out. "Where you off to?" he said.

I shrugged. "Just going home." I didn't reckon it was a good idea to tell him I was trailing a girl I didn't know. I had to be careful with PC Barlow because he wasn't that keen on me, to tell you the truth, and he'd pull me in if he got the chance. I never did anything big. Just messed about. Like the time I nicked a bunch of roses from some old biddy's garden to give to a girl I was having a thing for. The girl chucked them in the road and a few minutes later a car squashed them. Then another car. Then another car.

I was still counting cars when PC Barlow appeared. He said I'd end up getting myself locked away one day, and he took me down the station and put my name "on file." It would have cheesed me off except whenever PC Barlow was around I always got this picture in my head that stuff at home wasn't that great for him, so I never held a grudge or anything. Still, being "on file" was pretty bad news. I reckoned once you were "on file" you could get hauled in for anything.

Anyway, on that day he left me alone, and we were pretty close to Denton Drive by then, so I reckoned I'd seen the girl home safely. I felt good that I'd done that. I never had a sister—just one kid brother—but if I *had* had a sister I'd have looked after her like that.

As I left the castle path and turned into Station Road I blocked out the trouble with Billy and let Matt flood back in instead. When he came round, I'd dazzle him. I was sure I could put enough of a show together to get him really fizzing with interest. Although of course I was hoping it wasn't really the magic he would be fizzing for. I was hoping it would be me.

Kirsty clogged up my head all the way home. Billy would drop her soon—he never stayed with anyone for long—and maybe I'd bump into her at the castle when she was feeling down. She'd need a mate if she'd just been dumped. If I could get her to talk to me I could stun her with my witty and amazing conversation and she'd start to realize that—

"Where've you been?" Mum was watering plants by the sink when I walked into the kitchen.

I shrugged. "Nowhere."

She gave this sigh and kept on with the plants. One of them looked half dead. Brown leaves and straggly bits. It always gets me, seeing plants like that. It's like no one's ever cared about them properly.

I pulled a chair out and sat down at the table. Mark was in the corner, on the Internet. He was logged on to some space program and loads of planets and stuff kept whizzing about on the screen. It did my head in, just watching it. I guessed it was homework. Mark's only at juniors, but he gets loads of homework. I always reckon his school is like something off another planet. I'm glad no one had ever pushed to get me a place there.

Even Leigh Comp. is better than Mark's school. Just the blazers with the neat edge of stitching round the cuffs and collars are enough to make me want to vomit. Although I don't go much on the uniform at Leigh Comp. either. I'd hardly worn it when I was there. It got to me, having to wear the same stuff as everybody else, so I'd go in with a sports sweatshirt or the wrong trousers or something, and tell the teachers the puppy had eaten my clothes. Those teachers must have reckoned we got a new puppy every month. Although the truth was, we never had any pets. Not even a gold-fish. I was always sorry about that because I like animals. But anyway, that puppy eating the uniform stuff was early on. By Year Nine I'd stopped bothering with excuses.

"Trainers off! They're filthy."

I kicked them off, pushing them under the table with my feet.

"Sit on that chair properly. You'll break it." Mum dipped a cloth in the sink and began scrub-bing a tiny bit of mud off the tiled floor. It was such a minuscule bit of mud—you'd have needed a microscope to see it, but I didn't say anything. It's best to keep your mouth shut when Mum gets stressed about minuscule bits of mud.

I watched her as she turned back to trim off more dead leaves. "Where did you get that plant from?"

"Karl Reeve's grandmother has donated a box of them. We'll be selling them in the church jumble sale tomorrow. And there's a college prospectus in the hall. I think you should have a look at it."

"I can't go to college. You need exams and stuff."

"There are courses designed for people like you."

People like me.

"You need to focus. To get a view of the future." Mum put her hand up to her head as if she wanted me to know she had one of her headaches coming on. "You've got to do something with your life."

I suddenly felt achingly sad. That feeling you get at the end of a film when you know the couple aren't going to get together after all.

Mum walked over to Mark. He was still clicking away on that screen, an explosion of planets and stars and swirling gases looming out at him. Her face sort of smoothed out, and she rubbed his shoulders as he worked.

I rocked my chair up onto its back legs, letting it come back down with a crash.

Mum turned to me. "Your hands are covered in mud. You'd better wash them before dinner."

I went to the sink and turned on the tap really hard, so that the water shot out. It smacked down into the metal sink and drowned out the voices that were starting up again. I picked up that half-dead plant and turned the pot round in my hand. "Only a weirdo would want this."

"Someone will buy it. It's a nice pot, so just put it down."

I held it higher so it was face-level with me. It got to me, Mum saying someone would buy it because of the pot. I reckoned it was like someone only wanting to be your mate because you're wearing the right trainers.

"I've told you, Matthew. And turn that tap off. It's splashing everywhere."

I didn't answer. I got like that sometimes—not wanting to answer her. Actually I got like it a lot.

"Matthew!"

She was right behind and my hand sort of

jolted. I hadn't realized she was that near. There was this sudden crack. The pot collapsed in on itself, the plant dropping out and falling on its side into the sink. "Oh shit!"

"Don't talk like that. And I told you to put it down! You must have known what would happen. Everything always gets broken with you." Mum made it sound like I'd done it on purpose.

I picked the plant up again. The few leaves it had left were bent or broken. If it was sad before, it was suicidal now.

"There's no point keeping it." Mum huffed about, picking up the broken china and wrapping it in newspaper. "Take it outside and put it in the bin."

I went to get rid of it all, but at the last minute I didn't chuck the plant out with the china. I took it up to my room and put it in this lumpy old clay pot I'd made for some naff school project once. I fiddled with the leaves a bit, trying to make them curve out the way they were supposed to. I got the idea that it was looking better, sort of straightening up, but then the voices started. I didn't want to listen so I stuck on my Slack Daddy CD so that the thump thump thump would grind them away, and then looked out towards the castle.

I had Kirsty in my head again.

★

"Pick a card, any card. Don't tell me what it is." I was whirling around in front of Dotty, my dressmaker's dummy.

My mum's a dressmaker—or she was before she had the twins and Dad did his disappearing trick. Dotty used to belong to her. She lives in my bedroom now. I know it sounds a bit sad and geeky but Dotty makes a brilliant audience. I keep her dressed in jackets and shirts and bits of jewellery because it's good to have a life-size body to work tricks out on.

I don't tell Dotty anything though. I even keep my props out of sight. It's good practice for making sure I don't let anything slip when I'm with someone real. Magicians never give their secrets away.

". . . try and build the picture of the card in your mind. Then make that picture grow bigger. Brighter. Make it so it's really glowing. And when you're ready, I want you to try and pass that picture to me."

Dotty's headless, of course, so I had to *imagine* she was gazing deeply and intently, but that was okay. Imagining things has never been a problem for me.

"I'm getting something—it's coming through." I closed my eyes as if dazzling visions were blinding me. Then I snapped my fingers. "I've got it. The king of diamonds." I gave a deep bow to acknowledge Dotty's silent applause, but my mind was only half focused on what I was doing.

Matt. Matt.

Beautiful. Beautiful.

I turned away from Dotty and got a stack of *Gossip* magazines out from the box under my bed. I don't really like girls' magazines. They never seem to say much that interests me. But some woman had brought these round when she'd got stuck with them after a church jumble sale and I sometimes skimmed through them when I wanted a break from practising magic. This time I wanted more than a break though. I wanted help. Advice. I didn't want to mess anything up. I found an article called "LOVE AT FIRST SIGHT." It was all about eyes locking and skin tingling when you touch. It said that you feel as if you really really know someone, even though you've hardly spoken.

The whole idea of it seemed to shimmer. I hardly slept that night. I lay staring out of the window—I never draw my curtains because I love the night sky—and beyond the huddled roofs I could see the bones of the castle.

Matt. Matt. Thoughts swirled like shooting stars through my head. I remembered his voice and his eyes and the way that he'd smiled. Beautiful. Beautiful. I was already lost.

"What have you kept this for?" Mum pulled the curtains open and stood looking across at me with that plant in her hand. I was jolted awake, and for a moment I couldn't work out what she was going on about. I'd been in this sort of nightmare where I was watching that magician girl leave the castle. I started following her and as she reached the bridge she turned round to look at me. It was then that I realized it wasn't the magician girl—it was Kirsty—and her mouth was locked open in this silent scream. I was about to rush forwards and be amazing and heroic when Mum's voice sent the whole scene scuttling away under a stone in my head. I felt pretty sick though—like something terrible had been about to happen and I'd missed my chance to stop it. Outside, it was raining.

"I said—why have you kept this?" Mum was

dressed already. Smart. She wears her best gear just to stick the bin out.

"I dunno. I felt sorry for it."

"It's just something else to clutter your room with." Mum put the plant down again and picked my jeans up off the floor. "And why do you insist on wearing odd socks?" She was holding my socks like they were a couple of turds or something. I pushed my way deeper under the quilt.

"It's time you got up. Mark's already out. He's got a swimming competition and Karl Reeve's mum picked him up first thing. I'd have gone with them if the vicar hadn't needed me for this sale, but there just aren't enough people prepared to give up the time . . ."

I lay like a rock, listening to the rain. I was trying to bring back the scene with Kirsty, thinking I could still sort things for her, but the voices were buzzing and I couldn't think straight. Sometimes they just go on and on and I can't get away from them. I started humming, as a way of blocking them out.

"Stop that silly noise." Mum can't stand it when I hum. "You could help at the church if you're not doing anything else. We need someone to sell the raffle tickets."

That shook everything out of me. I was right back in the real world. What if I saw someone I knew? I stuck my head back out from under the quilt. "I'm going out."

"In this weather?"

"To someone's house."

"Whose?"

I had to think fast. Where could I say I was going? Suddenly, I thought of that magician kid. "I met this girl yesterday. She goes to Leigh Comp. but she's new and she's being bullied. I said I'd go and talk to her."

I watched Mum pick up the plant again, and examine it closely. "Who's bullying her?"

"Some of the sixth form lot from Leigh Comp."

I reckoned I was getting through. Being bullied was a big deal with Mum. She'd been up to the school a lot about it once upon a time, although it didn't get either of us anywhere. I learnt not to tell her in the end. It's best to keep your mouth shut about stuff like bullying.

"Where does this girl live?"

The answer stuck in my throat for a moment. Mum was likely to go into a major stress if I told her it was Denton Drive. On the other hand, it kind of fitted with the bullying idea. I decided to go for it. "Denton Drive. Number eleven, I think."

Mum held the plant at arm's length and narrowed her eyes. "I know that address. They've just moved there. The husband went off with a woman half his age after his wife had twins. Poor thing couldn't afford to keep up the mortgage. They're in emergency council accommodation."

I made a sort of grunting noise that I hoped would show her I knew all that, and more.

"We sorted baby clothes out for her at the last committee meeting. I tried to choose the best I could. It's a terrible thing to be left stranded with two babies." Mum put her hand up to her head, as if the whole idea of it was making it ache. "What's the girl called again?"

Big mistake. She'd expect me to know stuff like that. I screwed up my face, trying to make it look like the name was pushing its way up from under my skin. I used to do that at school, when a teacher turned on me for an answer to something. I used to pull my mouth all over the place and look up at the ceiling. In the end I'd make noises or say something naff that was supposed to be funny, just to break out of it. The teacher never got the joke, though, and I usually wound up staring at those walls again.

I got this flash of inspiration. "She did tell

me, but she was upset. Crying. I didn't catch what she said."

I reckoned I'd come up with the right thing. Mum was looking at me like there might be hope after all.

"I think it's Erin." She frowned. "Skinny little thing with long scruffy hair. The surname's Jones."

"That's it," I said. "Erin Jones."

I must have said it too fast because Mum lost that look of hope. "I'm not sure you should be going round there. I would imagine her mum's got enough to cope with."

"She . . . Erin . . . invited me. It'll be rough if I let her down."

And as I said it, I actually felt it. I wanted that kid to know that not everyone in Leigh Cove was a jerk like Billy Owen. Especially if her dad was gone and her mum was having a hard time and everything. I saw myself suddenly as a kind of Pied Piper for unhappy kids. Word would get out about me. I would be followed through the streets. Kirsty would watch me as I joked and laughed with an adoring flock, and . . .

"I'll be leaving at nine. Make sure you're up by then. And if you don't go to Erin's, I shall expect you at the church hall by eleven. And remember—I've got Mrs. Jones's phone number. It will be easy for me to check." Mum gave me one of her looks—the sort that said she could see inside me and would know if I was up to anything. Except she never could see inside me. I reckoned there were loads of things about me she just couldn't touch. Still, I decided it was a good plan to move the subject away from Erin and her mum.

"What will you do with that plant?"

"It doesn't look too bad. It seems to have made a miraculous recovery overnight. We might be able to sell it after all."

She lifted it out of my old school pot and went. It got to me, her going off with my plant like that. I'd sort of bonded with it.

I looked at the alarm clock and then dived back under the quilt. Half an hour before I had to make a move for Erin's place. Half an hour to try to get back to being an amazing hero with Kirsty again.

It was raining when I got up. At first I thought it was a good sign—he wouldn't have anywhere else to go. And then I thought it was bad—he wouldn't want to go anywhere anyway. Still, I had to be prepared. It would be better for me to be ready for him even if he didn't come, rather than risk slobbing around looking like the nightmare you can't wake up from . . . and then hearing that knock on the door.

The twins sounded like they were having their limbs amputated in the kitchen, so I went down to help Mum. Early morning, pre-breakfast, was a screaming time of day.

I put Lily on my shoulder and started leaping about. "The wheels on the bus go round and round, round and round, round and . . ."

"What are you doing this morning?" Mum shouted as she shook the bottles.

The wheels on the bus skidded to a halt. "Just . . . I don't know." I suddenly wasn't sure what to say. I'd never had a bloke round before. I'd never had a bloke full stop. I wanted to tell Mum, but part of me didn't want her to know. "Nothing much. I'm going to practise some tricks."

Mum nodded. "I finished making that white dove for you. It's behind the sewing machine, next to the ironing. I used old rags and wire for the body in the end."

Mum is brilliant about my magic. She

adapts all my clothes—even my school uniform. The gadgets I need are usually quite small. I don't have to be loaded down in order to be impressive. And I've always had a dream of being the first famous female magician. Most magicians are blokes. It's probably because real superstar magicians have to spend hours and hours on their own just practising. Blokes seem better at that. Girls are the ones who prefer to be in groups. Except me. Although not being in a group hasn't really been my choice.

"Give me Lily then," said Mum. "You get on with whatever you need to do."

I tweaked the invisible thread on the dove as I picked it up. The whole thing folded really small. I tweaked it again, and it fluttered open as if it was alive.

"This is brilliant. Thanks." I wiped gooey rusk out of Lucy's hair with a damp cloth and then went up to my room.

Ten minutes later I was flipping through a card trick, watching myself in the mirror. Watching myself is something I have to do. It's vital to know how I look. Sometimes I'm still standing in front of the mirror at midnight. Dad bought me a camcorder and when he was around he used to film me from all sorts of angles, which helped. I hadn't used it since he'd left.

Anyway, after a few minutes I stopped watching what I was doing with the cards, and started watching me.

I've never been that sure about my face. It's passable. I mean, I've got the right number of eyes and noses and mouths, but I'd never make cover girl of *Gossip*. I've got a sneaking suspicion that my mouth might possibly be too big, or my eyes possibly too small. Still, Tom Gray—who's in Billy Owen's tutor group at Leigh Comp.—says I've got an "interesting" look about me. Tom lives up the road and he catches up with me on the way home sometimes. He's hooked on photography and he's always taking pictures. He's quite sweet, and he can even be funny when he's away from everyone else, but I wasn't sure if his opinion about girls' faces counted for much. Still, I really liked him as a friend and at least "interesting" was something to work on.

I flicked through another *Gossip* magazine. They had a whole article on what to wear for first dates. "BE YOURSELF. NATURALLY."

I went with that. Natural was good. Except I thought I'd just nick a bit of Mum's mascara. I nearly poked my eye out with the wand, and I wasn't sure if it was the best thing for Matt to believe I naturally had lashes like crazed spiders, but if I stepped back from the mirror and squinted I didn't look too bad.

I might have dressed up a bit—I've got a couple of passable tops—but if I was going for a serious magic session I decided it was best to wear the big baggy sweatshirt that had come from the charity shop. Mum had sewn masses of secret pockets in it, so it was perfect. It's best not to use brand-new clothes if you're going to cut them about, and anyway this sweatshirt didn't look secondhand. Apart from a small stain on the left shoulder it seemed really new. The stain didn't bother me—Matt would be too busy watching the tricks to even notice—but it's amazing the things other people throw out.

I washed my hair twice. It dried sticking up the first time. I know washing my hair twice wasn't particularly "natural" but I caught a glimpse of one of those *Gossip* cover girls and started thinking that I had more chance of being picked to model for *Hedgehog Monthly*.

When I'd spent the best part of an hour getting "natural" I put on my Slack Daddy CD. I wanted Matt to know that even though I was younger than him, I was still into all the latest sounds.

I hadn't got a clue what time he was coming, but my possibly-too-small eyes could do gazing out of windows watching for him. I even quite liked the idea of it. We'd just done some of *Romeo and Juliet* at school and a group of us had rewritten the balcony scene in modern-day language. Kirsty decided Juliet should stomp about looking at her watch and say "Where the hell are you, Romeo?" She got a laugh from the rest of the group, and I laughed too, although I knew from when we did that play at my last school that "wherefore art thou" doesn't mean "where," but "why." Why are you called Romeo? Why couldn't I have fallen for someone else? I didn't correct Kirsty though. There are some things you don't let on about—especially not when you're new at a school like Leigh Comp.

So anyway, I set the scene with a morning

of uninterrupted gazing. I sat by the window, watching the rain puddle the dips in the pavement, and practised "interesting" expressions on my reflection in the glass.

It wasn't the scummiest house in Denton Drive. It wasn't great either, but at least there were no mattresses in the garden. Only nettles.

I banged hard on the door. I do that sometimes—bang hard on doors. I'm not that keen on doors that stay shut.

"Yes?" The woman that answered looked like she was being taken over by nettles too. Her hair was all tangled and she was wearing this manky grey dressing gown that you wouldn't even send to a jumble sale.

She was holding a screaming baby and I could hear another one grizzling somewhere inside the house. I had to shout. "Is . . . is Erin about?"

"Come in."

I was standing in the rain, half drowned, but when she said that I wasn't sure I wanted to go in. Even from the porch I could catch the whiff of pooey nappies and a vomity baby stench and I'd quite like to have legged it, but then I remembered the raffle tickets.

"Cheers."

"Erin!" Erin's mum shouted up the stairs, and then added in a softer voice, "Ssssh, Lucy. Sssssh."

She jiggled the baby about over her shoulder although it didn't make any difference, and then the other one upped the volume too. Erin's mum looked like someone who was being pulled in three places and I don't know why I did it but I suddenly held my arms out and said, "I'll hold that one for you if you want."

Erin's mum stared at me like I'd just grown an extra head or something, but after a second she handed the baby over and I was still stuck with her when Erin came down the stairs, wearing this huge yellow sweatshirt and waving a camcorder at me.

"That's incredible," she said. "You've got Lucy to stop crying."

As she took her off me I realized the sweatshirt was mine. Or at least it had been, until Mum got in a stress about a stain on the left shoulder and bagged it up for the Oxfam shop. It had really got to me, Mum doing that. I didn't mind Oxfam having it, but I hadn't given a stuff about the stain.

"You're so wet. Is it a long walk from your house?"

I muttered something about where I lived and then Erin's mum came back with the other baby. She took Lucy from Erin. "Your friend must have the magic touch." She gave me this smile like she reckoned I was pretty impressive, and went off upstairs.

Erin got my jacket and scarf off me, then led me past all these buckets and buggies into her kitchen.

"Do . . . do you want a Coke?"

"Great." To tell you the truth, I didn't. I tried to make myself think of that Pied Piper stuff, and how I was meant to be helping Erin and everything, but as she handed me the drink the whole pooey vomit thing started doing my head in and I just wanted to be gone. I'd go up to the castle. Hang about. Maybe Kirsty would turn up. And at least I *had* come here, if Mum ever pushed to find out where I'd been. "I'd better . . ."

"Hold on." Erin leant towards me, put one hand up behind my left ear, and held up this pound coin.

It was pretty slick and I was impressed. "How did you do that?"

She gave me this shy sort of look, but I could tell she was pleased. "Keep watching," she said.

★

He walked round the corner past the street lamp. Head down, hands pushed deep in his pockets, he was hunched against the rain. And still beautiful. Beautiful.

I watched him come through our gate and up to the front door, but I didn't go downstairs straight away. I'd been reading, "YOU WON'T GET YOUR GUY BY LOSING YOUR HEAD" so I decided that gambolling towards him like a puppy that's just heard its lead rattled was definitely out.

There was a knock on the door.

"Erin!" Mum really had to yell to be heard above the twins and Slack Daddy. I was embarrassed about the twins suddenly. I wished, just for that moment when Matt arrived, that they'd been asleep. And I was embarrassed about Mum, too. It would have been nice if she had at least been dressed and we'd managed to look like a normal, fully functioning family for five minutes. But we didn't. And we weren't. So at least he was getting an honest look at my life. And in a way that was what mattered. Deep down I believed that being truthful was about the most important thing anyone could be. If you couldn't be honest, you couldn't be any-

thing. I knew that because of the way my dad had been in the end. Not being honest just set up a chain of disasters that made everything impossible. I made a decision on the day Dad left that I would always always always be totally straight with everyone—whatever it did and wherever it led.

I decided to use the camcorder, because I suddenly panicked and wanted something in my hands when I first saw him. A sort of grown-up teddy bear. Stringing it over my shoulder I ran downstairs, trying not to look as if I'd spent the last two hours crouched by the window. Collapsing from lack of circulation was not high on the list of "TOP TEN TIPS TO ENTICE YOUR GUY."

He was holding Lucy. I thought it was amazing because he looked really uncomfortable, but she was gazing up at him and sucking her finger, which she hardly ever does for me.

"That's incredible. You've got her to stop crying."

As I took her off him I went gooey again, and I kept thinking how brilliant it was that he was standing in our hall with his hair dripping all over the carpet.

"You're really wet. Is it a long walk from your house?"

"I'm in Grange Avenue. The one at the end with the double gates."

I'd never been down there before, but I made a mental note to find out exactly where it was. "I'll take your jacket and scarf."

"Okay."

We sounded so stiff. So strange. All those whirling wonderful daydreams. I should have rushed into his arms. Melted into him.

Instead I just hung his things on the hook over mine. "We'll go through to the kitchen." I moved the breakfast clutter to one side. "Sit down. Do you . . . do you want a Coke?"

"Great."

Still stiff. We could almost have shaken hands.

I glugged out the Coke and as I handed the glasses over my fingers touched his. I got that buzz whizzing back through me. For a moment I thought I might dissolve into a blob again.

But then I saw him looking a bit uncertain, and panic caught me. Perhaps he wasn't enchanted by the crazed spider eyelashes.

Perhaps he'd noticed the stain after all. Distract. Distract. That was what I needed to do. "Hold on," I said, "you've got something behind your left ear." I stretched my hand towards him as I said it, and then drew away.

I was holding a pound coin.

It's really simple, that trick—once you've mastered sleight-of-hand. But Matt had those lit-up eyes and he was smiling. "How did you do that?"

I felt glowing and golden and glorious. I could write my own article for *Gossip*. "FIFTY MAGIC TRICKS TO MELT HIS HEART."

"Keep watching," I said. "Try and catch me out."

Erin blew me away with that coin, switching it into different hands.

She made a point of rolling her sleeves up, so I took a guess. "I reckon it's something to do with your sleeves? When you roll them up?"

She just laughed, showed me her two empty hands, then lifted my Coke glass. The coin was underneath.

"I don't get it. I haven't taken my eyes off you."

"It's only magic," she grinned, then frowned.

"I'll show you a few basics. I think I might have some cards around somewhere. Oh, look . . ." She suddenly produced this deck from out of nowhere. "Try these. They're smaller than normal cards. People don't notice the difference, but they're easier to work with."

I took the deck from her. "I've never been that great with my hands."

She watched me make a hash of it, and she was going on about false shuffles and stuff as I kept dropping the cards and having to start again. I didn't have a clue what she was on about, but I let her lean over and twist my fingers, pushing them into position. I'm never usually that keen on people pulling and pushing at me, but it felt okay coming from Erin. So okay that I even winked at her. I've never winked at anyone before. I mean it's a bit of a naff thing to do, isn't it? But it felt all right to be naff with Erin. She showed me other decks too, flicking them up out of thin air. She got one card to stand up on its own on the table. I just kept staring and staring at it and it looked so weird I reckoned she must have hypnotized me or something. Then she showed me this coin that was sort of glued to her palm.

"I can move my hand about any way I like, and

the coin won't fall . . ." She grinned at me. ". . . you can learn to palm all sorts of things. You can even use an egg." She flicked her wrist away, showed me her palm again—and there was an egg on it. Another flick and it had disappeared. It turned up bobbing about in my Coke. It was a real egg, too. Erin made me break it into a cup afterwards just to prove it.

I was feeling pretty buzzed up about all the stuff she was bringing out, and I reckoned it would be a laugh to try something for myself. "Teach me the card one you did with Billy yesterday," I said. "The one with the writing on it."

"Okay. First you get me to pick a card."

"Pick a card."

"Now tell me to write my name on it."

"Write your name on it."

She got a pen and wrote something. I couldn't see what it was, but she looked at me like we shared this amazing secret as she pushed it back into the deck. Then the door opened and her mum came in.

Erin looked round. "Are the twins asleep?"

Her mum sighed. "Just about. I think I'll nip out and—"

She didn't finish what she was saying before the grizzling started from upstairs. She closed her eyes for a moment, then shook her head. "I was going to say that I'd nip out for half an hour. I need some nappies from Shop'N'Save."

Erin went quiet, and her mum went off upstairs again.

I kind of twigged in to what her mum had been thinking. She wanted Erin to get the shopping, but she was too polite to ask me to leave. I'm good at that—working out what people really want even when they don't say it. "I need to get off anyway."

"You don't have to . . ."

"I'm going up to the castle." To tell you the truth, I was ready to get away. Now that the kitchen door was open the pooey vomit smell was hitting me again.

"I could record you doing that trick we were just practising."

"I've got to check out the bridge. It's got all this bad stuff round it." I don't know why I said that, to tell you the truth. I was just looking for excuses. Except as I said it my gut started churning and I remembered that nightmare and Kirsty and everything. But Erin latched on to what I'd said in a different way.

"You're right. The moat's a mess. I noticed it yesterday."

She got wound up about the whole thing, going on about all the rubbish and how we could do something about it. She was pointing that camcorder at me and to tell you the truth I suddenly wasn't that keen on having it stuck in my face like that. It made me want to get away even more. I started feeling pretty panicky, so I said, "You wouldn't want to stick your hand in that moat. You'd probably pull out a dead body or something."

She dropped the camcorder back down to her side and went quiet for a moment. I reckoned I'd probably upset her, but I couldn't think what to say to put it right.

"I'm glad you came," she said at last.

"Me too." I suddenly felt okay again. I *had* got a buzz from watching her—and it was stacks better than being stuck selling raffle tickets. I went to hand her cards back, but she shook her head.

"Keep them. I've got more upstairs."

It got to me, her giving those cards up. I mean, I knew they must be special to her. They were the tools of her trade, if you get what I mean. "Maybe I'll catch up with you again later?" I wanted to let her know that I'd had an okay time with her. And I reckoned it would be good for her, having someone around who would look out for her. I was back into that Pied Piper stuff.

She got that flushed face again when I said about catching up—so bright I reckoned it was only decent to look away. Instead I looked across at this photo on the shelf opposite. You could tell it was Erin even though she was only about three or something. She hadn't changed that much. Her mum was in it too, and a bloke with a beard. The bloke had his arms round both of them. They were in a garden somewhere. It was sunny. Masses of roses. No nettles.

Magic has always been a starry cloak for me to hide behind. People notice the tricks, and they don't notice me. The more magic I learn, the more I disappear. The invisible girl. But I didn't want to be invisible on that Saturday. I wanted Matt to notice everything about me.

"Let me show you something." I held the coin in the air. "I'm going to switch this from one hand to the other. Watch really carefully. It starts off in my left hand—" I held my palm open so he could see, then I closed my fingers on both hands. "I'm going to switch it from my left to my right. Look—

I'll even roll my sleeve up so you can see I'm not doing something sneaky with the cuffs or anything." A second later I showed him my right palm. The coin had switched.

Matt ran his hand through his hair, and shook his head.

"Watch again . . ." I switched the coin back, loving the baffled expression on his face.

"I reckon it's something to do with your sleeves? When you roll them up?"

I laughed, showed him two empty palms, then magicked the coin out from under his Coke.

"I don't get it. I haven't taken my eyes off you."

"It's only magic. I'll show you a few basics." I set my face to "interesting," and produced a deck of cards just by flicking my fingers, rattling on about special decks as I showed them to him. I've got different decks for different tricks. Being a magician is quite technical really. Logical. Organised. The real magic is to do with how well you can act. Or lie. Although I don't like to think of it as lying.

Matt took the deck I was holding out to him. "I've never been that good with my hands." Half the cards slipped down onto the floor as he tried to shuffle them. He had thin hands. Bone thin. Beautiful.

I moved my chair nearer and tried to get him to flick his thumb. "Once you've learnt the basic shuffle you move on to false shuffling. Palming. Cutting. Passing."

His hair had dried with a kink of curl in it. I could feel his breath on my cheek. Everything about him was electric, and I felt touched with something a million times more exciting than magic.

Then he looked straight at me, and winked. That really did it. He was so so gorgeous. I know my face burned, but I felt brilliant. I understood Juliet better than ever. My heart was behaving as if I was running a race, but it was a race I felt I was winning, so I kept talking. "You can learn to recognise different cards by touch. To make cards jump up out of the deck. To make a card stand up on its own on the table." I did that last trick as I spoke, and his eyes boggled.

I wasn't going to give away real magic secrets, of course—I hadn't lost it completely. I was sure he liked me—he was giving off all the right signs—but I wanted to make sure I kept on sparkling. "A HUNDRED WAYS TO KEEP HIM HANGING." The thing that mattered most was to make him want to see me again.

"Look at this." I held my hand up and waved it about. I had a coin fixed on my palm as if it was glued. "I can move my hand about any way I like, and the coin won't fall." I closed my fingers and he kept his eyes fixed on them as if he was trying to laser his way through to see what I was doing. "You can learn to palm all sorts of things. You can even use an egg." I opened my fingers again. The coin had transformed into a speckled brown egg. I made it disappear and then let him "find" it a second later as he went to drink his Coke. He was laughing. I was laughing. It felt brilliant.

"Teach me the one you did with Billy yesterday," he said suddenly. "The one with the writing on it."

"Okay. First you get me to pick a card."

"Pick a card."

"Now tell me to write my name on it."

"Write your name on it."

I got a pen, then picked out the two of hearts totally at random. It stunned me for a moment because I always used it as a special card. It's the traditional card of love. I was about to scrawl my signature when I stopped. Maybe it was a sort of fate, choosing the two of hearts. Maybe this was my big chance.

"DOES FATE HAVE A HAND IN YOUR FUTURE?"

Not that I really believed in anything like that, but it's definitely best not to walk under ladders. So instead of writing "Erin" I wrote:

"I like you. Lots."

I pushed the card back into the deck and the second I'd done it I went wobbly inside. I shouldn't have told him. It was too soon. But then I decided it was okay—I could get it back before he saw it. I'd just change the trick a bit and he wouldn't know what was going on. The kitchen door opened and Mum came in.

I realized it had gone quiet upstairs. "Are the twins asleep?"

"Just about. I think I'll nip out and—"

Only then the inevitable happened—a scraggy squall from the back bedroom. Mum closed her eyes. "I was going to say that I'd nip out for half an hour. I need some nappies from Shop'N'Save." When she opened her eyes she was looking at me, and I knew exactly what that look meant. She wanted me to go.

I felt trapped as she turned and went back upstairs. I hardly ever had friends round—and never since we'd moved. I thought Mum could have at least given me some space for that morning. I couldn't say "no" though. I didn't want to look mean in front of Matt.

"I need to get off anyway," he said.

Oh, bleak empty world. "You don't have to."

"I'm going up to the castle."

I turned the camcorder on and focused it, desperate for anything that would stop him from leaving. "I could record you doing that trick we were just practising."

He shook his head, drumming his fingers on his leg as if he couldn't wait to get moving. "I've got to check out the bridge. It's got bad stuff round it."

This was a chance to go up there with him. "You're right. It's a mess round there. I noticed it yesterday." I could look at him more closely through the lens. For longer. And without blushing. "Maybe we could clear it out." I wanted to add "together." Anything, anything, as long as we were doing it together.

"You wouldn't want to stick your hand in

that. You'd probably pull a body out or some-thing."

His face got this odd, panicked look for a moment, so then I panicked too. I'd pushed too hard. I should have waited for him to ask me to help. I switched off the camcorder. "I . . . I'm glad you came."

"Me too." He smiled then, but I still felt cold as I got his things from the hall. All that buzzing electricity was gone.

As he took his jacket, he held the cards out to me.

"Keep them," I said. "I've got more upstairs." It was only after I'd said that, that I remembered:

"I like you. Lots."

But it was too late. Again.

He looked pleased though, and I decided it was worth it. And anyway, what was wrong with him finding out how I felt? I was just being honest.

He pulled his jacket on, winding his scarf round his neck. "Maybe I'll catch up with you later?"

The bleak empty world exploded with colours again. He still wanted to see me. It was going to be all right.

Later, in Shop'N'Save, I added the latest copy of *Gossip* to the trolley. I read it when I got home, devouring it like it was a feast and I hadn't eaten for a month.

"LUSCIOUS LIPS GET HIM READY FOR LUV."

"NAIL POWER—HOW TO GET YOUR CLAWS IN HIS HEART."

"GET YOURSELF A CLEAVAGE AND BE HIS BOSOM PAL."

Rubbish. All rubbish. I flicked to the problem pages but they were just filled with anguished traumas about girls having a crush on their best mate's boyfriend, or their teacher, or some remote person who didn't even know they existed. It was all a waste of good trees. I chucked the whole thing under the bed with the rest of the pile. What I was feeling wasn't going to be anything cheap and shallow like that. I was going to be the heroine in a true-life love story. I would run barefoot through the night in a dress of white lace. I would stand drenched in moonlight, gazing mistily across the endless sea. I would dance among the stars.

What I was feeling was for real.

★

I crossed the bridge—walking like a kid trying not to tread on the joints in case it was bad luck—and went under the arch.

Kirsty and Billy were sheltering over by the east wall. They were smoking something, but they looked round as I went over. "What you up to?" Stupid question, but it just sort of came out.

"Playing tiddlywinks," grinned Billy.

Kirsty giggled, but she punched him at the same time. I reckoned it was her way of showing me she thought he was being a jerk.

I must have looked really geeky, because I was dripping wet from the walk up there, and I was still holding Erin's cards. I knew Billy would have to make some joke about them so I squatted down to click my fingers at Pox, trying to shove them in my pocket with the other hand. Pox started pecking at the laces on my trainers. I fixed my eyes on her, trying to make out that having a pigeon pecking at your trainers was the most interesting thing in the world.

"What's that?" Billy flicked ash down onto Pox's back.

"Just a deck of cards."

"Want a game? I'm a betting man."

"I don't go much on card games." I don't go

much on any games, to tell you the truth. I can never get my head round all the rules and stuff.

"So why have you got them?" Kirsty was looking down at me now. I got this idea, this horror, that I might have dandruff. Having some girl stare down at the top of your head is a way of making you start to wonder about stuff like that.

I straightened up, and Pox strutted off.

"Maybe we could play Snap." Billy put his arm round Kirsty and pulled her to him.

Kirsty jabbed him in the ribs. "Don't be so mean." She was laughing again, but I still reckoned she didn't think he was funny. I know what it's like, having to pretend blokes like Billy Owen are a laugh a minute, so I didn't mind.

I reckoned I should go for the truth. "That girl gave them to me. The one who was doing the tricks up here yesterday."

"Really? Are they rigged? Special corners nicked or anything?" Kirsty took the deck from me and flicked through them.

"I don't think so." It was doing my head in, having her that near. My voice was sort of croaky, and I couldn't meet her eyes or anything.

She flicked her hair away from her face and handed the deck back to me. "You shuffle them and then I'll pick one. We'll see if we can work this magic business out together."

"Bor-ing." Billy started kicking stones towards the west wall. "You want to keep away from that weirdo, Kirsty. He makes the hairs stand up on the back of my neck if he gets too close."

Kirsty looked at him and then looked at me, and then she shrugged and said, "Sounds like an interesting effect."

I could see Billy was pretty hacked off with her for saying that and from the look he gave me I thought I might have to leg it, but then he went over and shinned up onto the window ledge, sitting with his back to us.

I didn't want to shuffle the cards with Kirsty watching. "I haven't really got the hang of it yet."

"Come on." She tipped her head on one side and gave me this smile that knotted my gut. "Just give it a go."

I fumbled with those cards as if I had sticks instead of fingers. From the corner of my eye I could see Billy flicking bits of loose stone down into the sea. I reckoned he wasn't listening. Maybe I should just "give it a go." Maybe I should ask her if she thought I was okay. Whether I'd stand a chance if she wasn't with Billy. "I want you to pick a card . . ." God—what a geek. How could I ask her anything when I sounded like a frog with laryngitis?

She took a card from the middle of the deck.

"Look at it, then put it back in. Anywhere you like."

She slipped it back and I did another cock-up of a shuffle. ". . . And I'm going to ask you . . ." The words wouldn't come. It was like I was choking on them. I was getting so screwed up I forgot to keep an eye out for Billy. And then I felt this shove on one side. Billy's whole weight had bashed against me, knocking me sideways. I managed not to fall but my hand sort of shot out and the cards dropped through my fingers and down into the mud.

"Sorry, mate. It's so wet around here. I must've slipped."

I couldn't look at him—not him or Kirsty.

"Well, go on then, Magic Matt. Pick them up. Tell us which one was hers." Billy had lit another joint and the smoke from it was getting to my eyes. "We're looking for a show, Magic Matt. We're waiting for you to wave your wand and get a whole flock of doves flying out of your boxers." He stared at me, then down at the front of my jeans. "You have got a wand, I take it . . ." He laughed again, struck a match, then dropped it down onto the king of hearts.

I watched the burn spread across the king's face.

Then Billy grabbed Kirsty again. "Come on," he said. "Let's go. I've got a few tricks of my own to show you."

She took the joint from him, dragged on it, and closed her eyes.

Then they walked off, disappearing out under the arch together.

The king's face was sort of melting. Smoke curled up from the edges. The heart in the top corner seemed to be twisting forwards. I reckoned it looked like something in pain.

I found a *Gossip* article that Saturday morning. "MAKE THAT FIRST SNOG REALLY SIZZLE HIS SENSES."

"SIZZLE HIS SENSES." It was a stupid title. If I were an editor I'd have come up with something loads better than that. But I read it anyway.

I'd never thought much about snogging before. I'd heard Kirsty and some of the others going through gory details but I hadn't taken much notice. Now I wished I had. I needed to know everything I could. What did you do with your lips? Where did you put your hands? Just thinking about it made me go all twizzly.

I wanted it to happen and I didn't want it to happen. Or at least, I was scared of making a mess of it. But in "MAKE THAT FIRST SNOG REALLY SIZZLE HIS SENSES," it said that if you were with someone you really cared about, it would always be wonderful. And if he cared about you he wouldn't mind if you bumped noses or teeth. That made sense. It would be all right to do all that bumping if you both really liked each other. And if you didn't really like each other, you presumably wouldn't be snogging with them anyway.

I wondered whether Matt had snogged anyone before. That thought twisted in me. I wanted to be the first. The one and only.

I stamped on the king. I couldn't bear to look at it. I reckon I could've just lain down in that mud with those cards, and it wasn't a new feeling. It was old. As old as infant days. My papier-mâché monster being chucked into bushes on the way home from school. My sandwich box used to score goals with. My trainers stuffed down the loo. I just mucked about and made jokes and pretended it didn't matter.

Pox was pecking at the rest of the cards in the way that she'd pecked at my laces. I crouched down and stretched my hand out to touch her. She stopped pecking and ruffled her feathers. It hit me that her life wasn't great either, being up here on her own all the time. Cold. Wet. No mates. She should be hanging round in a flock or whatever it is pigeons did. It got me down all over again, thinking about it. I lifted her into the crook of my arm and after a moment I felt this kind of thrumming sound filling her up, and I knew she was feeling okay. And all at once I felt okay too. Stuff Billy Owen. I didn't want to lie splatted in the mud like a burnt-out king of hearts. Instead I began to pick up the cards, wipe the mud off them onto my jeans, and push them back in the packet.

One was lying a bit apart from all the others. The two of hearts. It had writing on it, scrawled across the middle.

"I like you. Lots."

I stared at it for a second.

And then it hit me. Kirsty must've written on

it while I was doing all that fumbling. While I'd been trying to say stuff to her, she'd been trying to say stuff to me. I had to let her know that I'd found it.

I raced through the arch after them and yelled, "I've got it!"

They were halfway down the hill, but Kirsty stopped and looked back at me. "Say again?" she called.

"I know what card you had just now."

Billy grabbed her arm but she shrugged him away.

She walked all the way back to the bridge and stood in front of me, really close. She touched her lips with the tip of her tongue. Was she going to snog me? Would she do that, with Billy watching?

"Go on then," she said.

"Go on what?" I had laryngitis frog throat again.

"Tell me the card." She laughed, her eyes dancing out at me like she knew what I'd been thinking. "You said you knew it."

"Two of hearts." I handed it to her.

She took the card and looked at it. Then she stopped laughing and her eyes locked into mine for a moment. She put her hand up and stroked my cheek really gently with the edge of her finger. Then she said loudly, I guess in case Billy could hear, "That was good. Really good. Almost better than doves coming out of your boxers."

Then she stuffed the card in her jacket pocket and was gone, chasing back down the hill to Billy. "He did it, you know. He got it right."

Billy grabbed hold of her and they messed about for a moment. At first I reckoned they might be fighting, but then I saw her arms go round the back of his neck and I knew that they weren't.

I stood staring at them. Why had she given me a message like that, and then been all over Billy again? She wasn't making sense.

But I could still feel her touch on my cheek. No girl had ever touched me like that before. In fact, apart from Erin that morning, no girl had ever touched me at all.

Matt didn't come back. Not all that first week. But the idea of him whirled through me. I can't describe what it did to me, just thinking and thinking and thinking about him. It was as if there was a circuit in my head and the thoughts went looping round it.

By Friday I was going nuts. English was our first lesson that morning.

"All right, everybody—we're doing descriptive writing today. I want you to imagine you are a minor character in *Romeo and Juliet* and, mimicking Shakespeare's rich and poetic style, give me one of the scenes from that minor character's point of view."

Mr. Nelson rose slowly up onto the tips of his toes, and then rocked backwards again. I was sitting near the front and I could see the hairs in his nostrils. Did people pluck nasal hair?

"Now remember—one of the tricks in good story writing is to ask yourself the question 'what if' . . . For instance, *what if* the nurse holds a secret grudge against Capulet? Or *what if* Benvolio owes a large amount of money to someone? What tangles can you wind your characters into? What problems can you give them to solve?"

I went for Gregory—one of Capulet's servants. What if Gregory was in love with Juliet too? What if Juliet didn't have a clue because she was so churned up with Romeo? My heart wasn't really in it though, and after writing the date and the title I was back on

Matt again. What if he really really liked me? What if he'd found I like you. Lots? What if he was thinking about me in the way that I was thinking about him?

"I've got to go early, Mr. Nelson. I've got a problem with my belly piercing. It's gone septic."

I shook myself out of the Matt daydream and looked up as Kirsty went over to Mr. Nelson. She stood close to him, one hand on her hip, pushing her hair behind her ear.

"Do you have a letter?"

"No, but I can show you." She slowly began to unbutton her blouse from the waist up.

Mr. Nelson went purpler than a beet-root. He did some frantic toe-rocking and muttered, "You'll need to catch up later. See me at breaktime tomorrow."

My eyes followed Kirsty as she went back to her desk and touched up her lipstick before stuffing her books in her bag. I could never even come close to looking like her, but as I watched her swing her way towards the door a new thought spun through me. Matt had liked me—fancied me—exactly as I was. Kirsty had the luscious lips and the "claws in his heart" nails and a cleavage to die for, but Matt hadn't chosen to spend last Saturday morning with her. He'd come to see me. I could be who I was with him, just the same as I didn't need him to start being lead singer in a band or captain of the football team. Although I thought I would still get some lipstick . . .

"Miss Jones?" I looked up again, trying to ignore the nasal hair. "Your pen seems to be having major difficulties moving itself across the paper. Perhaps you could encourage it a little by picking it up."

Now it was my turn to get a beetroot face. I didn't usually get into trouble at school. I launched into the Gregory writing without stopping. What if? What if? What if? I was just at the point of getting him to lurk behind the curtains in the balcony scene, when the lunch bell went.

Tom caught up with me in the corridor. "I heard stories about you doing magic tricks up at the castle."

We walked towards the dining hall. "I do magic wherever I can. I love it."

"I know how you feel. I love photography like that too. And I've got some great shots of the castle. Maybe I'll show you them some-time."

"Sounds good." I shifted my bag to the other shoulder as we headed for the cutlery trays. Holding a spoon up in front of him, I rubbed the handle. "Do you think that's clean?"

"Seems okay. Why?"

"Look at it more closely. Really concentrate."

"It still seems—oh, no—it's moving. Bending. How are you doing that?"

"In fact . . ." I handed it to him. "It's bent so much that it's snapped."

Tom was shaking his head, but he had the lit-up eyes as he took it from me. We got our pizzas and sat down opposite each other. He held the spoon up in the air, as if a better light would make it make sense. "I don't get it. It's stainless steel. How can it have bent and broken?"

I grinned and did my "deck of cards from nowhere" routine. "I'm going to flick these past you. Choose one. Just don't tell me what it is yet."

He laid the broken spoon on the table in front of him as if it was a jewel to cherish always and forever and looked up. "Okay."

I handed him a pen. "Write down what it was."

He wrote on the back of his hand.

"Show it to me now."

He held his fist up. "Six of diamonds."

"Now check your back pocket."

He looked at me as if I'd just asked him to stand on his head and whistle the theme tune from *Neighbours*, but he checked anyway—and pulled a card out. "The six of diamonds? I just don't get it. You're incredible."

I bent him another spoon. And a fork. And then a spoon again. I would have done a few more but one of the dinner ladies started weaving towards us between the tables. "Got to go," I told Tom quickly. "Take care."

"Will you—?" he said, but I didn't stop to hear the end. A good magician always knows when to leave the stage.

"That college prospectus is on the table. There's a form with it. You need to apply by the end of the month." Mum picked up this naff crystal swimming trophy that Mark had won at the weekend, and started dusting it.

I sat down at the table and watched my alien brother fiddling with the deep-sea diving watch that Mum had bought him because he was so clever and fast and could beat the stuffing out of his best mate in a swimming pool.

I'd got given his old watch. Mum stopped buying me new ones because I kept breaking them. I didn't mean to—it's not like I had a shower in them or anything. But they just always ended up going too fast. Or too slow. Or not at all.

I picked up the prospectus but I couldn't read it. I can never read anything for long. The words go all weird and I get pictures in my head of people writing them—the authors, I suppose. So instead I wondered what Kirsty was doing, right that second. It was Saturday afternoon, so she was probably with Billy. It did my head in, thinking about her being with Billy.

I looked up at Mum. She was still faffing with that cup, looking like getting it so bright you could light a tunnel with it was the most important thing in the world. Mark, still faffing with his watch, looked the same.

It got to me suddenly, watching them. They were like a couple of puppets, their heads nodding, and their hands moving at the same time. I got this idea that I wanted to leap up and start jumping round the room like someone on strings. I stopped myself though. That was the sort of stuff I'd done at school when things really did my head in, and to tell you the truth it never went down very well.

But I reckoned, as I watched them, that Mum and Mark had been carved out of the same piece of wood. Or hatched from the same alien egg.

And thinking like that gave me this crashing down feeling deep in my gut, and I didn't want to look at them anymore.

The doorbell jolted me. "I'll get it."

"No, you won't." Mum squinted one eye at the crystal swimming trophy. "You've got that form to fill in. Mark can go."

Mark got up, pushed his chair in carefully, and went out to the hall. I reckoned they must all have to put their chairs in like that at alien school.

He was back in a moment. "It's for you." He sat down and put his watch on again. Then he looked up and made this kind of "alien who's just discovered a new life form" face at me. "It's a girl."

My gut twisted. A girl. A *girl*. It had to be her. Kirsty. Oh, Christ. *Christ.*

Mum shook her head. "You're not doing

anything until you've filled in that form. You'll have to tell her you're busy."

I got up slowly. I even pushed my chair in, alien-school style, and then went to the door practising this cool "good to see you" expression.

"Hiya."

The "good to see you" expression froze. It wasn't Kirsty. It was Erin.

When Matt hadn't turned up by lunchtime the next Saturday, I just sort of lost it. Mystic Melissa said it was a bad week for sudden decisions, but I wasn't about to let Melissa shape my life. And all that stuff in *Gossip* was rubbish anyway.

I found the house easily. I remembered the gates. But I walked round the block twice even though it was pouring with rain, just trying to pluck up the courage to go down the long gravel drive.

I might have gone round a third time, but I suddenly saw Billy and Kirsty coming towards me. It was just the push I needed.

There was nothing in the world as scary as having to walk past them. I pushed open the gates and scrunched up to Matt's front door.

★

I liked Erin, but I didn't think it was that great to have her turn up unannounced. I mean, I know I'd gone to her place, but she'd invited me. Not that I'm bothered about stuff being arranged, but it kind of got to me that day, the way she stood on the doorstep wearing this naff lipstick that made her look like a kid dressing up. Which was a slimeball thing to think, and I was sorry a second after I'd thought it.

But what if Kirsty really did come by? What if she saw Erin standing there and got the wrong idea? What if, because of Erin, I missed my chance?

"I've got a new trick. I've come round to show it to you."

"I . . . I'm busy. I'm writing something." I reckon it must have been the first time in my life I'd ever said that to anyone.

Erin looked as if she'd come to a party and found she'd turned up on the wrong day. I felt even more of a slimeball then. And I remembered I was supposed to be the Pied Piper looking out for her and everything. So then, even though I didn't want to, I said, "But I've got five minutes," and I let her follow me through into the kitchen.

"Erin!" Mum gave her this sort of churchy smile, like she gives to old biddies at jumble sales. To tell you the truth, there's loads of stuff Mum doesn't understand about old biddies at jumble sales. They're not always what you think. I can remember one year I watched one go round with a huge shopping basket, nicking stuff. I never told anyone—I mean, what was the point? But it gets me the way old biddies are meant to be good, and young blokes like me are meant to be bad. I reckon helping yourself to a few crummy roses is nothing compared to cramming your bag with stuff that's raising dosh to save the sick and starving.

I looked at Mum. "Erin does magic tricks. I thought Mark might like to see some."

It was pretty inspired, me saying that. Mum would be torn between getting Erin out so I could get on with that form, and letting Mark have a bit of a treat. I reckoned Mark would win, and after Erin had finished I might be able to get out and up to the castle before Mum caught on. If I went up there often enough, one day I was bound to catch Kirsty on her own.

Mum was still beaming the churchy smile. "Magic tricks? That sounds interesting. Can I get you an herb tea, or a fruit juice?"

"Fruit juice, please." Erin sat down.

"So—what have you been practising?" I put on this keen and interested sort of voice.

"I'll show you—but I'll do it on Mark, if Mark doesn't mind." She started shuffling her cards, laid them face up on the table, then looked across at Mark. "Could you pick a card for me? Just hold it in your head. Don't tell me what it is. Oh—and I gave my real deck of cards away to a friend last week . . ." She shot this smile at me like we shared another big secret, then gathered up the spread of cards, "so I'm going to have to ask you to use your imagination." And then—without her seeming to have done anything—that whole deck disappeared. Instead she fanned out this invisible deck and held them out to Mark. He had a weird expression on his face. I couldn't make it out for a moment, and then it hit me—he actually looked like a proper kid. Not like someone in an alien school who gets up early every Saturday to win crystal swimming trophies. A proper kid doing kid-type things. And I got that crashing down feeling again then because I thought that even though we were so different, neither of us had done much of being a proper kid ever.

Erin was looking at Mark. "Can you see your card?"

He shook his head.

"Let me cut them a few times. It might help." She made this movement with her hands as if she was cutting a deck. She was good. Amazing. It looked like she really was holding something. And suddenly—out of thin air—she was. The two of hearts. That blew me away a bit because it was the same card Kirsty had written stuff on. And then, as she turned the card round to make sure I'd seen it properly, it disappeared again—and a white dove fluttered up from nowhere. It wasn't real—I don't reckon I'd have liked it if she was using a real bird—but it looked pretty impressive. And even Mum clapped, although I knew she'd be faffing around later to get all those feathers up the vacuum cleaner.

Erin still hadn't finished. She turned back to Mark. "Do you know what time it is?"

Mark glanced down at his deep-sea diving watch—only he didn't glance down at his deep-sea diving watch, he glanced down at his bare wrist. The watch was gone. He looked at Mum and Mum looked at him and I could see their "hatched from the same egg" brains ticking although they couldn't work out what the hell had happened.

"Could you just check your back pocket a minute?" said Erin.

Mark stood up and pushed his hand in his pocket, then his whole face sort of boggled like he'd come up from under the sea too fast. He pulled his hand back out. He was holding his watch.

It was a killer. Mark's face. Mum's face. Probably mine, too.

I grinned at Erin.

She grinned back at me. "It worked."

"I'll come over again and let you show me some more." I reckoned I would too. Maybe I'd learn how to magic birds out of thin air for Kirsty.

"I've got a new trick. I've come round to show it to you."

He stood in the doorway, his hair all sticking up and his clothes crumpled. He was wearing odd socks and he was beautiful. Beautiful. "I . . . I'm busy. I'm writing something."

There was something in his voice. Something guarded. I felt it as much as heard it and my excitement crashed in the centre of me. I'd messed it up.

"But it's okay. I've got five minutes." He stepped backwards, opening the door wider. His hall wafted lemon air freshener.

The crashing stopped. He was just awkward. He wasn't sure how to talk to me. Maybe he didn't have many girls calling for him. If that was true it was brilliant as far as I was concerned. I should learn to toughen up. Stop thinking the worst every time. I followed him through into the kitchen.

"This is my mum, and this is my brother Mark."

Matt's mum was shock number two. She was the *Gossip* jumble sales woman. I remember she'd turned up with the vicar and they had bags of baby clothes and potties and things like that. I'd hated all that charity so I'd gone up to my room and put on Slack Daddy really loud just to drown the whole thing out.

She looked like she was off to a wedding in her cream dress and pearl-buttoned cardigan. I wondered if Mum was dressed yet.

"Erin does magic tricks. I reckoned Mark might like to see something."

"That sounds lovely." Matt's mum glanced at my wet footprints squidged across her mirror-bright floor and gave me a disinfectant-clean smile. I gave her one back.

His brother was pressing buttons on his watch and looked up at me shyly. There was a picture of him on the wall, looking really serious and dutiful in a posh blazer and cap. I looked round to find one of Matt, but I couldn't see any. Instead there was another picture: a small print of *The Last Supper*—the bit at the end where Jesus washes everyone's feet. The Jesus in this picture was really lit up and glowing and it made me think, for a moment, that maybe Jesus might have been some sort of a magician. All those miracles and everything. Just suppose, when he was little, that Mary had sewn secret pockets into his robes? And Joseph could have taught him to make special wooden apparatus like the "Inexhaustible Box" or "Magic Dice." Although they probably didn't have dice in those days. But anyway, by the time Jesus grew up he would have been a whizz at it. It wouldn't be that hard to turn water into wine—I could probably work out a trick that's similar. And lots of people will believe anything. Not me, though. For a start, I didn't believe in God much. I had prayed a few times, mostly when Dad first went, but God never seemed to be taking any notice. I suppose it's a bit much to expect, if you don't believe in him, but in my darkest hours I would have given God a chance if He'd managed to come up with some sort of solution.

I blocked out Dad and the darkest hours and wondered if Matt's mum would have liked people to wash their feet before they walked across her floor.

"Can I get you an herb tea, or a fruit juice?" Matt's mum was already filling the kettle.

"Fruit juice, please." Was that what Matt drank? It was hard to imagine. In fact it was hard to imagine Matt fitting into this bright polished house with the bright polished mother and the bright polished brother. I started wanting to hug him again.

"So—what have you been practising?"

Matt's voice still had that guarded edge and I wondered, just for a second, whether he was trying to hurry me along. I just about managed to stop myself sinking into squelchy quagmires of panic again.

"I'll show you. I'll do it on Mark, if Mark doesn't mind."

I didn't particularly *want* to do it on Mark

but I was scared I might get that electric shock feeling if I got too close to Matt. I needed to stay calm—on the outside at least.

"Could you pick a card for me? Just hold it in your head. Don't tell me what it is. Oh— and I gave my real deck of cards away to a friend last week . . ." I glanced back at Matt as I said that.

I like you. Lots.

Then I rattled on, ". . . so I'm going to have to ask you to use your imagination."

That trick was brilliant. Or at least, what I mean is, they all seemed to think it was brilliant. I flicked between real cards and invisible ones. The white dove fluttered up out of nowhere, soft white feathers drifting down onto the floor. At the finale I "magicked" Mark's watch into his own pocket and he looked as if I'd just flown him to the moon and back. But the most brilliant thing of all was Matt's face. He was so lit up after I'd finished. More glowing than the Jesus in the *Last Supper* picture.

I went to see Erin that Monday. I'd already tried the castle but Kirsty wasn't about. She clapped her hand over her mouth when she saw me, and it got to me in a good way, so I grinned. "Am I that much of a shock?"

"Sorry. No. I . . ." She looked over my shoulder. "I thought you were going to be Kirsty Carter."

That knocked me back a bit, to tell you the truth. "Why?"

"I just—I saw her earlier. Coming back from school. I thought she might call here."

Erin was sounding sort of embarrassed, and I got this idea it might be something to do with me. Maybe Kirsty had gone on about that card in class or something. Girls always seem to talk about stuff like that. "Do you know Kirsty then?"

"She's in my English group." Erin took my jacket and scarf and I followed her into the kitchen.

"Do you talk to her much? At lunchtime or anything?" It hit me that they must be in the same year, although Erin looked way younger than Kirsty.

"Not much. Hang on. I'm going to get something."

She disappeared for a moment, then came back carrying this book. It was called *Modern Magic* but the cover looked like it had been made out of dinosaur skin, if you get what I mean.

"This is what I started with. My d—someone bought it for me from a secondhand book shop when I was six. It's got basic tricks and history and everything. Look—it goes right back to ancient times."

She started turning these yellowed pages and I made grunting noises like I thought it was amazing, but I was getting pictures of some old bloke with weird hair faffing around, magicking coins under cups and it was hard to concentrate.

Erin was pretty fired up about the book though. "There's always been magic in the world, hasn't there? Think about sages and wise women and Indian fakirs who turn sticks into snakes. Or what about the Bible? Moses and that burning bush, for instance. Any decent illusionist could make that happen. I mean—even Jesus and all his miracles . . ."

I couldn't really follow what she was going on about, so I asked her, "Does she—is Kirsty with Billy a lot?"

"I think so. I don't know what she sees in him though. She could get someone loads better."

Erin closed the dinosaur-skin book, spun these gold-backed cards out of thin air, and handed them to me. "I want to show you some-thing different. These four cards have ancient symbols. Sun and moon. Fire and water. Choose one and put it on the table with the other three on top, while I keep my eyes shut. You can even cover the cards with my magic book so I can't see them at all."

"Okay. Done it."

"Now think about the card you chose. Make the picture in your mind grow bigger. Brighter. Make it so it's really glowing. When you're ready, I want you to try and send that picture to me."

She sat and stared at me. I wasn't that keen on being stared at like that, to tell you the truth.

I went for the water, but I couldn't make it big in my mind. Kirsty was taking up all the space. I wanted to keep talking to Erin about her but I couldn't work out how much she knew. I reckoned I should tread carefully. "Can you imagine having a bloke—you know—someone you fancied—but you didn't know how to make it happen?"

Erin got this look on her face like a rabbit with a stick up its backside. "Maybe."

"Would you do anything special to get him to notice you?"

"Like what?" Her voice went sort of uncertain, like she wasn't sure where all this was going.

"I dunno. Tease him and stuff. Do girls do that?"

"Some might. I wouldn't."

I suddenly got this feeling I'd hit a sore point and had been putting the boot in. I felt like a slimeball then. "Sorry. I just—I wasn't sure how girls did things." I shrugged, to let her know it wasn't a big deal.

She stared down at her dinosaur-skin book, like she'd rather look at that than look at me. I was gutted that I'd upset her. "I'd better go."

"Will you come again tomorrow?"

She still sounded pretty hacked off. It made me even more certain I'd opened my mouth and put my size ten right in it. Maybe she had some bloke back at her last place that she'd never got over or something. I mean—she looked young to me and I couldn't picture her with a boyfriend but I didn't really know her, so I sort of muttered, "Maybe."

"Only maybe?"

"Okay—definitely."

There was this silence, like neither of us knew what the hell to do next.

And then she said in this small voice, "Oh, and by the way . . . your card was Water."

I grinned at her then. Whatever had gone wrong, we were on track again. "You're great. You'll have to amaze me even more next time."

She grinned back. I reckoned she was feeling okay when I left.

That Monday, as I was walking past the train station, I saw Kirsty. She was waving wildly, so I waved wildly back.

I felt stupidly pleased that she was making so much effort. Normally she just ignored me. I even started to walk across to her. But then I realized she was looking past me—to where Billy was hanging about near the station entrance. She hadn't been waving at me at all. She'd been waving at him. What an idiot I must have looked. Dark ghouls of embarrassment howled through my head for the rest of the way home.

When I got indoors I went straight upstairs and put my Slack Daddy CD on really loud. That was it! I could never go out again. I'd spend the rest of my life shut away in my room. I wouldn't eat. I wouldn't speak. I'd just huddle in the corner with my back to the closed curtains while spiders spun cobwebs through my greying hair.

I flicked through a deck of cards, watching them blur as I shuffled faster. Faster.

Faster. Downstairs someone banged on the front door.

Faster. Faster. I would be a world record card shuffler. Not that anyone would ever know, because I'd only ever do it in my room . . .

"Erin," Mum called. "It's your friend for you."

Faster. Faster. It must be Kirsty. She'd realized about the waving, and she knew I'd be feeling terrible. She was nicer than I'd thought. People always were, once you got to know them. Or at least, that was what Mum was always saying. But could I face Kirsty right at that moment? What would I say? What if I ended up looking even more pathetic?

"Erin!"

"Okay. Coming." I stopped the manic shuffling, picked a set of my extra special cards from Dot's pocket, and went downstairs. I'd show Kirsty the trick while we were talking and she'd be so impressed she'd blaze my name round the school. Everyone would want to know me. Everything would be all right.

I hit the bottom stair and then stopped.

It wasn't Kirsty. It was Matt. *Matt!!!* I clapped my hand to my mouth. Brilliant brilliant brilliant. The way things happen when you don't expect them! Kirsty faded into a haze of nothing.

He grinned at me. "Am I that much of a shock?"

"Sorry. No. I . . . I thought you were going to be Kirsty Carter. I saw her earlier. Coming back from school. I thought she might call here." I stopped then. I didn't want to spill out the bit about my idiotic waving. "GIRLS WHO TELL ALL DON'T GET TO THE BALL."

"Come in. Give me your jacket. Are you okay?" It all came out a bit gabbly but I was buzzing.

"Do you know Kirsty then?" he said.

"She's in my English group." I poured him a Coke.

"Do you talk to her much? At lunchtime or anything?"

"Not much." I didn't want to talk about Kirsty. I wanted to show him things. Tell him things. But I didn't want to do the trick straight away. I didn't want to be someone who just sort of danced on stage every time I saw him.

Then I had a brilliant idea. I'd show him the roots of what I did—let him see it from a different level. "Hang on. I'm going to get something." I raced upstairs to my room, then raced back down again. "This is what I started with . . ." I fingered the pages of *Modern Magic*—my most precious ever book. Dad found it in a secondhand shop when I was about six. Opening the cover had been like opening a door into another world. I couldn't read much then, but I fell in love with the illustrations. Detailed line drawings of hands shuffling cards; elaborate carved boxes with secret compartments; mechanical masks with switches and levers. Dad would read out the tricks to me at bedtime. The names were brilliant too. The Feast of Lanterns. The Vanishing Canary. The Flying Watches. The whole book was a golden key into another world. I handed it to Matt. "There's always been magic in the world, hasn't there? Think about sages and wise women and Indian fakirs . . ."

"Does she—is Kirsty with Billy a lot?"

"I think so. I don't take much notice of her." It wasn't exactly true, but I wasn't going to let him know that I thought she was beautiful and fascinating and wished I was more like her. I didn't want him thinking about her instead of me.

I closed *Modern Magic*. I realized I couldn't just hand him the key. He'd have to want to look for it for himself.

I decided to do the trick on him that I'd planned for Kirsty. Get his interest that way. "I want to show you something different. These four cards have ancient symbols. Sun and moon. Fire and water." I handed them to him. "Choose one, put it on the table with the other three on top, while I keep my eyes shut. You can even cover the cards with my magic book so I can't see them at all."

"Okay. Done it."

"Now think about the card you chose. Make the picture in your mind grow bigger. Brighter. Make it so it's really glowing."

I was looking into his eyes. He was looking into mine. "When you're ready, I want you to try and send that picture to me."

All that gazing. I hoped I wasn't going to go all red-faced and ridiculous.

He kept his eyes on mine but there was an

edge to his voice, as if he was struggling with something. "Can you imagine having a bloke—you know—someone you fancied—only you didn't know how to make it happen?"

Fireworks exploded inside me. He didn't want to talk about magic. He wanted to talk about us. There was an edge to my voice too. "Maybe."

"Did you do anything to get him to notice you?"

"Like what?"

"I don't know. Tease him and stuff. Do girls do that?"

Perhaps he wasn't sure what I felt. Maybe I like you. Lots. wasn't enough. I should have written You're fantastic and wonderful and I've never met anyone like you before in my entire life. Except I would have needed a bigger card. "Some might. I wouldn't." I made my thoughts bigger and brighter and really glowing. Read my mind. Read my mind. Read my mind.

Time stretched. He breathed. I breathed. The fridge gurgled. Any minute now. Any minute now. I was certain that sizzling snog was about to ignite.

Only at the last minute he drew back and

looked away. "Sorry. I just—I wasn't sure how girls did things. I'd better go."

I sagged. I crumpled. My mind whispered, "You're fantastic . . ." My voice said, "Do you want to come again tomorrow?"

"Maybe."

My mind whispered, ". . . and wonderful." My voice said, "Only maybe?"

"Well, definitely."

My mind whispered, ". . . and I've never met anyone like you before in my entire life." My voice said, "Oh, and by the way, your card was Water."

His voice said, "You're great. You'll have to amaze me even more next time."

Next time. Next time.

I went to the castle after I left Erin.

Kirsty was there, sitting by the wall on her own. I know it was my big moment to be witty and amazing, but my brain seized up. "What you been doing?"

"This and that." She didn't look like she was switched on properly, if you get what I mean.

"Are you okay?"

She shrugged.

I stood next to her and tried to look casual

and relaxed although the voices kicked in again and I got scared that I was going to have to start humming or something to drown them out.

I started talking, just as a way of putting a block on that humming idea. And I wanted to move stuff on—say something that mattered—so I sort of blurted, "You know that card? The two of hearts?"

Her eyes focused slowly and she looked up and gave me this faint smile. "What about it?"

"I just wondered if you . . ." I wanted to ask her if she'd meant it—if she'd *really* meant it. And I wanted to tell her it was the same for me. Only I was still faffing about trying to get the words out when there were footsteps on the bridge and Billy came through the arch.

"Where the shit were you? I told you to wait by the station while I got sorted with Nathan."

Kirsty took a long time before she answered him, like it was hard for her to shift her thoughts from me to him. "I felt rough. I needed the air up here."

"Well, you should have effing well said. I could've got busted hanging about looking for you."

They stared at each other and it was like I wasn't there. "Did you get it?" she said at last.

"Yep."

She went over to him, leaning her head on his shoulder, and I didn't want to watch. I was about to turn away but suddenly I saw this shadow on her and I got this feeling of something bad—something terrible—coming. It was like this black shape hurtling down towards her and she was facing the wrong way so she couldn't see it. I wanted to start shouting and tell her to move but another bit of me knew that shouting would be even worse than humming, and anyway she wouldn't listen. The whole thing got me pretty churned up and I started pressing my hands against the wall just as a way of not looking at her. I grazed my knuckles and didn't realize that they were bleeding until Billy said, "You jerk. You into self-harming or something?"

I tried to face him out then, but he just laughed and shrugged like I wasn't anything. After a moment he and Kirsty went off together without even glancing back at me. I stood staring after them because I could still see the shadow on her, but I tried to tell myself it wasn't anything real. Just stuff in my head. And then a few minutes later the sky started chucking it down with rain and the cold got to me, so I went home.

When I got in, Mark had his crystal swimming trophy on the kitchen table and he was looking at it like it was the best thing he'd ever had.

"Mum's in bed. She's got a headache."

"So what's new." I hung about behind him. I was feeling pretty keyed up, like I didn't know what to do with myself. I opened drawers and shut them. I picked things up and put them down again.

I got this box out of one of the drawers. I knew what was in it—cash from the church jumble sale. I counted it. Over three hundred quid. I remembered my plant and wondered what it had gone for. Or had some old biddy stuffed it in her shopping bag? I picked out a set of spoons. They were silver. Special. Passed down from Gran. Mum only used them on her churchy coffee mornings. A bunch of women with plummy voices would sit around our table talking about God. I sat in on one once and asked what they reckoned would have happened if Jesus had got let off at the last minute. If he hadn't been crucified and he had just grown old and died. It was in my head that if that had happened maybe no one would have remembered him much at all.

I was buzzing with questions about it but they

weren't that keen on listening to me, and I could tell they didn't think it would have made such a good story. Mum said it worked out like that because it was what God had planned and her mouth went into this thin line, which was her way of saying she wasn't going to discuss it anymore. In fact they all seemed pretty hacked off with me.

Remembering it made me wish I could gate-crash one of those churchy coffee mornings again one day. I'd show up with Kirsty and we'd muck around like she did with Billy. That would give them something different to talk about.

As I thought about Kirsty again, I started flicking one of the spoons in the air.

"Stop it!" Mark sent me an alien stare. "They're Mum's best spoons. She'll go nuts if you break one."

"You can't break spoons. They're metal."

"You should still put it down. You might scratch it or something."

"Get it off me then," I said.

I wasn't looking for trouble but I had stuff in my head about what Kirsty might be up to with Billy and it was doing me in. I wanted distraction. Mark got up and started trying to snatch the spoon. I caught him in an armlock and he began kicking and shouting so I gave him this shove—

not really hard or anything because I didn't want to hurt him—but he fell forwards and thwacked against the table. The table did this sort of wobble, and the crystal swimming trophy wobbled too. I went to grab it but I couldn't move quickly enough. It smashed down onto the kitchen floor.

"What's going on in here? I'm trying to get some—" Mum stormed through the door.

"He pushed me. I was trying to stop him messing about with your spoon, and he pushed me." Mark started making noises like a seal being culled. "I've got to give that trophy back next year."

Mum turned to me. "Look at the trouble you've caused again."

"It's always me you get at, isn't it? What about Mark? Why don't you have a go at him, too?"

"Because Mark is . . . different. Easier." She wasn't strung up now. She looked sort of tired. Like she was sagging. "Perhaps if Alex . . ."

"Alex? My dad? Perhaps nothing. He doesn't even keep in touch. Not even a Christmas card. So don't go shoving him in my face just because it suits you."

"I'm not shoving him in your face." She stood

and stared at me for a moment, as if there was stuff she was trying not to say.

I was on a sort of roll and I couldn't stop. "He legged it when Mark was just a baby and to tell you the truth I wasn't even sorry. He never took much notice of me anyway. And you two were always fighting."

"Everything was difficult. Stressful."

She started rubbing her forehead and closing her eyes. "We thought that having Mark would make things different. Make things all right."

"So they weren't all right with just me about? I wasn't enough?"

I waited for her to say of course I was enough. They'd just wanted more children. There was nothing wrong with wanting two kids.

But she didn't say that. She stared at me for a moment, then turned away like I was something she didn't want to look at. "I can't think straight at the moment. Leave me alone."

That got to me too. I mean, she'd only seen me for about ten seconds. And all that stuff about wanting to be alone wasn't true because she wasn't getting Mark to go away. Just me.

A voice I hadn't heard before sort of whispered in my head. I hadn't been enough. I hadn't been enough.

I chucked the spoon down on top of the smashed-up trophy and stamped on it, feeling the glass scrunch into splinters under my trainers.

Stuff Mum and stuff Mark. Stuff them stuff them stuff them.

He didn't turn up on Saturday. When he didn't come in the morning, I thought he'd come in the afternoon. Then it moved into evening. By nine o'clock the bleak empty world was closing round me again.

"It's just you and me," I told Dotty at last, floating my lipstick above my palm. "This is my newest trick. What do you think?"

Dotty didn't think anything.

Outside, the rain hurried at the window. I pressed my nose against it and screwed up my eyes. The light from the street lamp danced strangely. Suppose he was ill? Suppose he was lying in bed pale and weak and whispering my name through bloodless blue lips.

I ran downstairs and into the front room. "I'm going out."

Mum looked up from watching *Saturday Superstars*. "Not this time of night."

"I'm not a kid."

"You know I don't let you walk the streets

when it's dark. Especially not round here."

"Well, why did we move here then? Why did you bring us somewhere that's heaving with mad axe murderers?"

I didn't wait to hear how it wasn't her fault and it wasn't her choice. I pounded back upstairs and turned Slack Daddy up so loud that the house rocked.

A minute later Mum hammered on the door. "Turn that *down*! You'll wake the twins."

I snapped out the sound and sank onto my bed. I would suffocate in the dark folds of sorrowing silence.

The next thing I knew, Mum was standing by the bed, holding Lucy and looking down at me.

"You've slept with your clothes on all night. Are you ill?"

I sat up, feeling fuzzy and furry. "I must have dropped off." I rubbed my eyes with the back of my hand. Yesterday's mascara smudged across it. "Have you got Matt's phone number?"

"It's on a piece of paper by the telephone. His mum left it there when she brought the baby things round, in case I needed to contact her about anything." Mum prised Lucy's fingers off a beaded necklace she was wearing. "She's been very good to us. Very supportive and understanding."

I thought about Matt's mum in her pearl-button cardigan and wondered how she'd cope with the twins honking up all over her. Although she'd had two boys. She must have had to deal with it once.

I went downstairs and found the number, tore the paper into small neat squares, and then magicked it together again. Then I let it hover above my palm while the phone rang.

And rang.

And rang.

Mum passed and stopped to show Lily the floating paper. Lily's fingers stretched out to grab the telephone cord.

"I'm wasted here, my audience just doesn't appreciate me," I said, catching the paper in my hand and scrunching it up. When I opened my palm again I was holding a beaded necklace.

"Very clever," said Mum, taking it back off me.

The phone still rang. And rang.

"They're probably at church," said Mum.

I shook my head. Matt's mum and Mark might be, but Matt wouldn't. Maybe he'd just staggered bravely to the phone. Maybe he'd been about to pick it up when his legs gave way and he collapsed in the lemon-fresh hall.

I let the phone ring for ten minutes, went upstairs to shower and dress, then went back down and rang for five minutes more.

Nothing.

I couldn't bear it. "I'm going out," I called to Mum, grabbing my jacket.

"But you haven't eaten." She came into the hall, mashing fruit into a saucepan with a fork.

"Not hungry."

"And it's raining. Pouring."

"The old man's snoring." I opened the door.

"I still don't think . . ."

From behind her, in the kitchen, the ritual limb amputation was beginning.

"See you," I said. And I went.

Ringing the bell, I peered through the mottled glass of the door, trying to see if I could make out a body on the floor. I couldn't. Then I began to think that perhaps he was at the castle. I could go down Station Road and hang around a bit. I didn't want to go up there on my own, but I thought I might be lucky and bump into him coming back. I saw Tom outside Shop'N'Save, and swerved away quickly. He was trying to balance an umbrella and load a film into his camera at the same time, so he didn't see me. I was glad. Matt might feel awkward about coming over if I was with Tom.

By two o'clock I was soaked and shivering and caught up in a new daydream that Matt might have called while I was out. The idea got stuck in my head like a scratched CD, and I was running by the time I reached my gate, dodging round a beaten-up red Nissan car that was parked half on the pavement. As I pushed through the front door I heard voices in the kitchen. Lily and Lucy were squealing, but I could tell it was a bloke's voice, and he was talking to Mum. Well, actually, Mum was laughing. He'd come. I'd known it. I must be psychic.

I looked a mess, all soaked and soggy and

my hair stuck to my scalp, but I didn't care. I swung into the kitchen.

"Hello, sweetheart," said Dad.

The way things happen when you don't expect them.

My face went more rigid than a mechanical mask. "What are you doing here?"

Dad had Lily on his lap but he got up and came over to me. "I know I should have rung, but I was passing and . . ."

Passing! Passing! Like we were people he'd met on holiday one year and he had just discovered the address in the bottom of his coat pocket.

My mechanical-mask face said, "I don't want to talk to you."

Mum was making coffee in Dad's old mug. In the baby chair next to her Lucy was gurgling as if she'd just been chosen to star in *Chuckling Cherubs*. Lily was drooped over Dad's shoulder, her eyes half closed, sucking her finger dreamily.

"I'd like to take you out sometimes. Maybe for a McDonald's, or to the cinema."

"Why don't you take your new girl-friend?" The mechanical-mask face snapped its mouth shut.

Mum put Lily in the chair next to Lucy, and came and took Dad's arm. Why was she touching him like that? It was as if he was the one that needed protecting. "Leave it for now, Chris. We'll talk later."

"About what?" My mechanical-mask eyes rolled a glare over them both.

Dad wasn't giving up. "I care about you."

"Well, tough." All of the levers clicked and clamped as I gave him one last look of steel then ran upstairs, crumpled down on the bed and pulled the duvet over my head. Go away. Go away. Go away.

Ten minutes later I heard the front door open and a car started up, rattling away down the road. Mum knocked on my door. "I know it's hard, and you're bound to be angry. I'm angry too. But I want to hear what he's got to say."

"You were laughing." How dare she be laughing. How dare the twins be all cherubic and chuckling.

"I wasn't laughing when I opened the door and saw who it was. I was as upset as you are."

I rolled over so that my back was towards her. "Is he coming again?"

"Yes."

"Well, you're stupid then." I said it low, so I wasn't sure if she'd heard me or not. From downstairs Happy Hour with Daddy seemed to have ended badly and the twins were starting to cry. Mum squeezed my shoulder, and then went back to them. I scrunched my pillow up and slammed it down onto the bed again. She was stupid. Stupid stupid stupid.

"DON'T LOSE YOUR DIGNITY WHEN YOU'RE DUMPED."

I stayed in my room for all that weekend, just playing Slack Daddy over and over. I had it up pretty high because I needed to blot out the voices. They seemed louder, like someone had opened the door to their room.

Slack Daddy blotted out Mum, too. I didn't even hear her call to say she and Mark were off to swimming, or to church. But then maybe she didn't call.

Late Sunday morning I turned the music off and lay on my bed like I was this zombie or something, just staring at the ceiling. The way Mum had looked at me. The way she'd looked away. I wasn't enough. I'd never been enough.

I had this sick vomity feeling about the whole

thing, and I didn't want to move. Didn't want to think.

The phone went twice. Someone came to the front door. Stuff them all. I wasn't talking to anyone.

Mum did try a bit, coming in with trays of food. "I'm sorry." She turned as she was carrying away the untouched Sunday dinner. "Maybe we should talk . . ."

It scared me, her saying that, especially with her voice all sad and everything, so I cut her off. "I'm busy. I'm going to Erin's."

I sat opposite Matt at our kitchen table. "Have a look at this magic box."

He seemed quiet and distant and I wanted to reach him in whatever way I could. He took the miniature box from me and traced the carved wood pattern with his finger. "Looks great. What's it for?"

I handed him a small silver key. "Open it. Can you see it's got three tiny dials inside?"

"Yep."

"Right—now I'm going to turn away, and I want you to set the dials to three numbers—anything you like. Just tell me when you're ready."

I turned away. I liked this trick. Dad had

bought it for me off some auction he'd found when he was surfing the Internet at work. I think it must have been quite expensive because it was so tiny and compact, and no one would ever know how complicated it was inside.

"I've done it."

"Okay. Now lock the box."

"Done that, too."

I turned round and gave him a long look. "Hold the numbers in your head. Make them bigger. Brighter. Make them so they're really glowing."

He held his eyes on mine. I could get lost in this. Lost in him.

"Three hundred and thirty three," I said.

My getting it right jolted him. "There's no way you could have guessed that. It's like that other mind-reading one you did—the one with the water. Go on. Tell me. How do you do it?"

I grinned. "It's so simple. When you find out you'll kick yourself. But magic—real magic—isn't just about clever tricks. It's about creating a mood. Building a fantasy."

"How d'you mean?"

I pulled a pen from the air and let it float

horizontally between my opened hands. "This is a special pen."

"Can I look at it?"

I handed it to him. After a moment, he handed it back. "I don't get it. It looks normal to me."

I grinned. "It is. You have to watch more closely."

I let the pen float again, and he frowned. "I still can't . . ."

"I always carry around my own pens, eyebrow tweezers, nails, nail files. Things like that. I keep it all small stuff, so it's easy to hide." I magicked a collection of my "props" from out of his jacket pocket—all things I wouldn't normally have dreamed of showing anyone. But I didn't care. I was racing ahead with all the secrets I could give away. Handing out the precious gems I'd been gathering for years.

"Look carefully at these. You can learn how to give them magical powers too—if you don't mind me stitching a few 'extras' into your jacket. Then we can work on sleight of hand, and ways to catch the imagination of your audience. You have to get them to think you can work miracles." Slowly I brought my hands together so that the tips of the pen touched my palms.

Matt came very close.

Closer. Closer.

Concentrate. Concentrate.

"I think it's amazing. You're amazing. But the sensible bit of me knows it can't be real." He leant back in his chair. "Are there people about who believe it is?"

You're amazing. You're amazing.

Concentrate. Concentrate.

I tried to keep my voice steady. "More than you'd realize. People *want* to believe in magic. They don't want to know about the springs and the magnets and all the other clever gadgets." I began closing my palms together as if I was going to pray. Matt's eyes boggled as the ends of the pen pushed out through the backs of my hands, making it look as if they were skewered on it. I opened them suddenly, letting the pen clatter down onto the kitchen floor. "Look." I held my palms out for him to examine. "No blood."

"Okay. You got me. I believe. I reckon you can probably walk on water, too." He grinned—the first time he'd smiled all evening. "It must be really something to have people think stuff like that about you. But scary, too."

"Why scary?"

He shook his head. "You'd have to make sure you never started to believe it yourself. If that happened, you'd be bonkers."

"It wouldn't happen. Every trick is practised and practised. If you started to believe it, then I suppose you *would* be bonkers." It was wonderful, talking to him about magic, all my thoughts and ideas tumbling out. "Next time you come I'm going to really get inside your head." I know I was glowing as I rattled on. "I'm going to see what you see. Feel what you feel. Tap into your tomorrows."

"Sounds good." He grinned again. "I'll be round when you get in from school."

"And . . ." I held the box out to him. "Have this, too. Keep it. You get this little card that goes with it—that's the bit you keep palmed in your hand."

He frowned down at it and shook his head. "I'll never work it out. I'm no good at stuff like this." I watched him open the box and fiddle with the dials again. Then he glanced at the card. His frown cleared, and his expression was like a light turning on. "Is that it? Is it really that simple?"

"Probably everything in the whole world is simple. Once you know the way it works."

I leant forwards and dangled a wallet—his wallet—in front of him.

He checked his back pocket, then shook his head. "You're always way ahead of me. D'you reckon you could teach me just a bit of it?"

I was floating on air. There was so much to show him. More and more reasons for us to spend time together. And that was what I wanted. All my time tangled hopelessly with his.

It was a Tuesday—over a week later—when I went back to the castle.

I remember it as a crazy day. One of those days when the sea is black and wild and the gulls go mad, like they all know something is going to happen and they keep trying to tell everyone, only no one has a clue what the hell it is they're on about.

Crisp packets and paper and boxes and bottles were being chucked about by the wind. Pox strutted over to me so I knelt down and let her flap onto my shoulder. Then I pulled myself up on the west wall window ledge and watched the waves slashing about underneath. The drop was pretty steep and I got the idea of falling. It sort of gripped me for a while and I let the wind smash into me. I was still feeling pretty down about that stuff with Mum and everything, although she hadn't tried to talk to me about it again. And I didn't want her to.

Pox fluttered down from my shoulder and I sort of woke up, which was pretty lucky. I stroked her head. "It's okay," I told her. "I'm just messing about. I'm not going to let myself fall." Although to tell you the truth, I might have done. Just in that moment, I might have done.

I thought about Kirsty instead.

I like you. Lots. I like you. Lots.

I got a picture of her coming across the bridge and in through the archway. I ran it through my mind. Made it bigger. Made it brighter. Made it so it was really glowing. I started on this fantasy that she'd turn up and watch me without me even knowing she was there. She'd see me sitting with my back against the cold stone, staring moodily out to sea. Moodily. It would be an okay thing to be sitting moodily. Like a rebel hero in a film.

Pox settled into the crook of my arm and I got Erin's cards out, flipping through them and showing her this trick where you could get four aces to come out at the top of the deck, even when it looked like they'd been put in the middle. Pox stuck her head on one side like she was taking it all in. I reckoned she was the best audience I was ever likely to get. I was about to give her a bit more of a show with one of the pens Erin had sewn into my cuff, but then I looked round and saw Kirsty standing underneath the archway, leaning against Billy.

"You've lost it." Billy was chewing gum really fast, as if he was in a gum chewing competition or something. "You've been talking to that poxy pigeon, and laughing."

"Just running through a few tricks." I'd wanted to say it in this cool, I-don't-give-a-toss-about-you sort of voice, but it didn't come out like that. It came out laryngitis frog throat again.

I got hold of Pox and slid down from the ledge, stumbling at the bottom. I had to grab at the wall, so I made a big show of sticking Pox on my shoulder as I straightened up, making out I'd meant to land like that.

Kirsty came over. "It's good the way Pox sits on you. I wish she'd do that for me. Can I hold her?" She cupped her hands and I stooped and let Pox slip down onto her palms. I hoped she wouldn't flap about. I wanted Kirsty to think that holding Pox was something great.

And it worked. Pox settled on Kirsty like she'd never sat anywhere better in her life. "It tickles. Her claws." Kirsty laughed. I hadn't seen her laugh. Not properly. It gave me a buzz, seeing her all sparkling and everything, so I laughed too.

"You have a go, Billy. See if she'll sit on your shoulder like she does with Matt."

"That effing bird is as weird as he is. They're kindred spirits." Billy spat his gum out on the ground, scuffing up stones with the edge of his trainer.

Kirsty slid him this flirty sort of look. "Come on. It's sexy seeing a bloke master something wild."

That really got me. Did she think that about me? Sexy. Not that you could call Pox wild.

I like you. Lots. I like you. Lots.

Kirsty went right close to Billy and raised her hands. Pox shuffled onto Billy's shoulder. She looked okay about it, even though he was still scuffing and jiggling about. I'd taught her to feel safe doing stuff like that.

Kirsty gave Billy that same slanty-eye look. "I wish I had a camera. I—oh, my God—no . . . !"

She clapped her hand over her mouth and laughed again, really creased-up this time. "She's shat on you. There's a big white splodge all down the back of your jacket."

I'd seen Billy switch moods but I'd never seen his face change like it did then. The whole look of him scared the hell out of me.

"Bloody bird!" He grabbed Pox, then he lifted his hand high over his head.

I moved to stop him but it was like my body was ten seconds behind my brain. I heard Kirsty shout.

And Billy chucked Pox in a high arc towards the west wall.

I don't believe in God or stuff like that, but I prayed then. This fast race of words sort of zapped through my head. Let her be all right. Let her get herself out of this. Let her fly. The God I don't believe in wasn't listening. Pox hit the wall with a thud. She dropped to the ground, her beak locked open and her one eye staring up at the sky.

Billy walked over to her, looked down, and then laughed. He laughed a lot. Just laughing and laughing, like it was the funniest thing that

118

had ever happened. Then he went back to Kirsty. "Let's go."

Kirsty shook her head and pushed him away. "Leave me alone."

He took some more gum from his pocket, unwrapped it, and flicked the foil paper into the air. "Okay. I've got to settle with Nathan for tomorrow's gear anyway. I'll come back for you later."

"Don't bother," Kirsty muttered.

But he'd already gone off whistling through the archway. I don't reckon he heard.

At the front of the room Mr. Nelson rocked on his heels as I went to my seat. "We're carrying on the piece with your minor characters again today. Remember to keep asking yourself the question 'What if? What if?'"

I stared out of the window. Matt had come round every day since that Sunday, and I'd shown him loads of ideas. What if we started performing together? Once I'd left school we could maybe get a job on a cruise ship and travel the world. We'd make a brilliant team. What if our name spread so far we began to . . .

Mr. Nelson's shadow loomed up. "Can I check your pen, Miss Jones?"

I handed it to him and he held it in the air, scrutinizing it with one eye closed. "Ingenious and enchanting. A pen that writes with invisible ink."

"What d'you mean?" For a moment I thought I must have slipped up and given him one of my "special" pens by accident.

"What d'you mean, *sir*." Mr. Nelson's nasal hairs quivered.

"What do you mean, sir?"

"I mean that, according to your English book, you haven't done any work at all this morning. Now there's a whispered secret echoing in the school corridors that you're touched with magical powers. It seems even the school canteen have had to take measures to counter the dark forces that you wield."

I stared down at my English book while the eyes of the whole class burned into me.

"So let's see if I can get this instrument to work a bit of magic for me too." He took the pen, leant over me, and scrawled four words across the middle of the page. "See me after school."

"Seems to do the trick." He rocked back on his heels and turned away.

After school. After school. I hoped he wouldn't keep me too long. After school was a Matt time of day.

If only.

If only I hadn't come up to the castle.

If only I hadn't let Kirsty take Pox.

If only I hadn't taught Pox to be so tame.

All that went through my head. Billy had done it, but it was my fault.

It was Kirsty who knocked me back to where we were.

"What are we going to do?" She was crying and I put my arm round her—just as easy as that—as if it was normal. She pressed her head into my shoulder, like I'd seen her do with Billy. "I guess I'll have to bury her," I said. Her hair smelt of oranges mixed up with rain.

She'd stopped crying but she had this voice like she'd gone empty inside. "We buried my cat when he got run over. A fox dug him up."

I pulled her closer and stroked her hair.

She looked up at me. "You're so s—" She hesitated.

I hesitated too. Well—more like locked up. I

was waiting for her to say "stupid." I was sort of ready for it. Like waiting for a punch on the jaw and knowing you're not going to be able to dodge away.

". . . sweet," she said.

Then she took my scarf off, pulling it slowly. Her fingers touched the back of my neck. I could feel her breath on my skin. "I'm not used to blokes being sweet. Not boyfriends. Not my dad. Not any bloke before." She was whispering, flicking the scarf lightly over her own shoulders. "And there's something special about you. When I see you I get this feeling that—I don't know—that everything might be all right after all." She got hold of my hands and squeezed them. "You even feel different to most blokes." She traced the shapes of my fingers. "It's as if you're buzzing with something. Tingling."

Tingling wasn't exactly the right word. It was more like I was on fire. And suddenly I was kissing her hair, pulling her against me and whispering stuff although I didn't even know what the hell I was saying.

I'd reckoned she was with me. I'd reckoned she was part of it, if you get what I mean. But then I realized she'd sort of frozen up. She started jabbing her elbow into my gut. "I thought you liked me. I thought you might be someone I could get to know like a proper friend. Bloody blokes. You're all after the same thing." She started crying again.

"Look—I'm sorry. I wouldn't hurt you. I didn't mean . . ." I was useless. I was geeky and clumsy and I'd loused the whole thing up. I couldn't look at her and she couldn't look at me so I went over and knelt beside Pox, trying to stop myself shaking.

Pox was so still. The whole business of being dead hit me then. The way something can be moving and thinking and feeling and then it's just over. Everything finished. And then I was crying too, these tears landing on Pox alongside the rain. Her feathers got dark and sticky. The whole world was crap.

I looked back at Kirsty. "I won't let the foxes get her. I'll put her in the sea." I wiped my face. "I'll let her go from the ledge. It's almost a straight drop from there."

I shinned on to the ledge and balanced as best as I could. The rain was really going for it and the wind got under Pox's feathers and made her look sort of fluttery. I noticed for the first time that she was touched with shimmery green in among the grey and I remembered all the times she'd perched on me and followed me about and pecked my laces. This was doing me in.

"Hurry up," Kirsty sniffed. "I can't stand it. Just do it."

I started whispering just to tell Pox I was sorry even though I knew she couldn't hear. I kept on and on and all the time I was trying to get the guts to throw her and get it over with, but I couldn't. I just couldn't. And then everything went quiet. I thought maybe Kirsty was calling to me but it was like she just kept opening and shutting her mouth and no sound was coming out.

The wind and the rain and the sea and the gulls were blotted out, and it struck me that maybe the world had ended and I'd gone into this sort of limbo place where nothing was real. My hands burned and I could hear the voices and I got the idea they were telling me something, although I didn't have a clue what it was.

And then normal things started seeping back and Kirsty was rattling on about me looking odd. "You're swaying," she said.

I slid down from the ledge and stood in front of her. I felt a bit out of it still and it was hard to keep steady.

"You didn't do it." Kirsty put her hands on her

hips. "You'll have to put her in a hole and a fox will get her after all."

"I won't have to do anything like that," I said. "Look at her."

"I don't want to."

"Look at her."

"You're scaring me."

"*Look* at her."

Kirsty dropped her eyes down to where I was holding Pox out in front of me in both hands. Then she pressed her knuckles against her mouth. "You jerk. You've been playing a trick on me. You're not right in the head. It's just like Billy said. You're a weirdo. Weird weird weird."

Weird weird weird.

I didn't watch her as she ran away under the arch.

I just stood for ages looking down at Pox, who was looking back up at me with her one good eye.

Alive.

"So you didn't come up with a spell to get you out of detention then?" Mr. Nelson looked up from marking, and then glanced at his watch. "The quicker you write, the quicker we can both go home."

What if Gregory gets more and more obsessed?

What if he does something terrible because he's so jealous?

I flicked through my copy of *Romeo and Juliet*. Shakespeare's words made me giddy, and I whispered a line aloud: "Love is a smoke made with the fume of sighs; being purged, a fire sparkling in lovers' eyes." I leant back in my chair and closed my eyes. Matt. Matt. Matt.

"Nearly your bedtime, Miss Jones?"

I jolted and started writing. What if Gregory rushes in at the end to save Juliet? What if she refuses to let herself be saved?

I scrawled the last sentence and put my hand in the air. Mr. Nelson didn't look up.

"I've finished. Sir."

He didn't answer.

Did teachers go on courses to learn to be like this? I got up and went and stood by him. He still didn't flicker. He just kept on scrawling ticks and crosses and caustic comments. I put my head on one side to try and read what he'd written, and noticed that watch again. It would be easy. So easy . . .

"You've pulled the rabbit out of the hat then, metaphorically speaking?" Mr. Nelson's voice cracked like a gunshot and I jumped back guiltily.

"Sorry? Sir."

He nodded at my book. "Leave it on that pile. If I'm lucky the fairies will tiptoe in and mark it overnight. Do you believe the little people might lend me a hand like that, Miss Jones?"

"I don't believe in that sort of magic. Sir." I closed my book up carefully and added it to the top of the pile. Then I collected my things and raced out of the classroom. I had to get away from Leigh Comp. as quickly as possible—before Mr. Nelson decided to check the time again.

Mum was waiting for me as I pushed open the front door. "Go into the kitchen. We need to talk."

I walked through the hall. Lily and Lucy were asleep in their bouncer seats, their heads slumped onto their chests.

"Sit down."

"I'm not a dog."

"You can stop the clever talk. I had a

phone call just now from your English teacher."

I should have known. Why had I risked it? "So?"

"He says you've just had detention with him and while you were there his watch mysteriously went missing. From his wrist."

"It was just . . . a joke."

"Not a very funny one, Erin."

"It's on his desk, inside my English book. He'll find it quite quickly."

"He'd already found it. That was how he was sure it was you. But we had a bit of a chat."

"What about?"

"About how you ended up with detention in the first place, for instance. What your work is like. Who your friends are."

"So?" Again.

"I didn't know much about the friends you see during school time, but when I told him you'd been seeing a lot of Matt he was very concerned. He told me Matt was . . . well . . . everyone always had big concerns about him. He was always in trouble when he was at Leigh Comprehensive."

I picked a spoon up off the worktop and

made the tip of the handle curl round to meet the front. "Matt just doesn't fit into rules and timetables and everything that's boring."

"What's got into you, Erin? You didn't use to be like this. You used to be such a nice girl."

"You're saying I'm not nice?"

"No—I didn't mean that. But the moods. The make-up. I think perhaps . . ." Lily woke up, grunting and punching the air like a miniature boxer. Mum unstrapped her and picked her up. "Matt doesn't seem to be doing you any good at the moment. It might be better if you don't see him. At least for a while."

"You can't stop me from seeing him. You'd have to tie me up and lock the door and put poisonous snakes round the outside of the house and—"

"Leave it, Erin. I *can* stop you and the more you go on like this, the more I can see that I need to."

"How will you stop me?"

"I'll think of something. I'll talk to Dad."

"Dad? What has he got to do with anything?"

"He's still responsible for you, and he still cares about you."

I dropped the spoon down onto the worktop. It spun full circle and then clattered onto the floor. "He cared so much that he dumped us all and ran off with some tart with her hair still in bunches."

Mum closed her eyes for a moment, then looked at me again. "He's trying to put things right. He's making an effort."

"Well, he's too late. Why does he think he can just come back whenever it suits him? And why do you let him?"

"Don't push me, Erin. I've got enough to deal with."

Lily's grunts turned to a grizzle, and then a scream. Lucy woke up and joined in. And then I was screaming too. I hated her. I hated Dad. The twins. The house. The garden. The grass. The leaves on the trees. The invisible molecules in the air. Mum listened in a hunched up, hopeless way, as if I were throwing rocks at her.

I don't know how long I would have gone on for if the phone hadn't rung. I swung away into the hall and picked it up.

"Erin?" Matt's voice.

I was shaking and crying, but I managed to speak. "Hiya."

"Can you meet me at the castle? I'll wait for you on the bridge."

"You sound terrible. Are you okay?"

"Yes. No. I just need to see you."

Mum passed me, a twin in each arm, as she went up the stairs. I pressed myself against the wall so I didn't have to touch her. She didn't even look at me. "I'll be there as quick as I can," I whispered into the receiver.

I slipped out of the house. Mum didn't see me, and I wouldn't have cared if she had. Matt wanted me. He'd said he needed to see me. He needed to see me. He needed to see me.

I had Pox tucked in my jacket when I got home. I couldn't have left her up there waiting for Billy to come back and finish the job. I got this idea I could maybe make her a sort of shoebox nest and keep her in the shed, but Mum caught me going out through the back door of the kitchen.

"What are you up to?"

I reckoned I should come clean. I mean, I could hardly keep Pox a secret forever, so I unbuttoned my jacket to show her. "She's been shaken up," I said. "She needs looking after." To tell you the truth I didn't get what had happened to Pox after Billy had thrown her. Maybe she'd just been stunned. Or maybe she'd been playing dead or something. But, whatever it was, she seemed to have got over it. In fact she seemed pretty good. I held her in both hands and she was looking at Mum with her head tipped on one side and I reckoned Mum would at least feel a bit sorry for her even though she was never that keen on pets and stuff.

Mum rinsed out a cloth and started wiping down the worktop surfaces. "Not here, Matthew. We can't have a bird here."

"Not in the house . . ." I started to try and sell her the idea of the shed and the shoebox. ". . . she'll be outside and . . ."

Mum went on to scrubbing at the doorknobs on the cupboards, rubbing them so hard it was like she was entering a doorknob cleaning competition or something. "It would mess on everything, and bring germs into the house. If it's really injured, perhaps we could contact a bird rescue society. Pass it on to someone who knows what they're doing." She was still scrubbing and rubbing and not looking at me.

I stared out into the garden. The rain blew in

through the door, sort of blasting into me. And suddenly I wanted to go over that "not enough" stuff again. It was like it was prickling through me like a devil dancing about.

"You had to have Mark because I wasn't turning out the way you and Dad wanted. That was it, wasn't it?"

Mum sort of jolted, like I'd just given her an electric shock or something. "Please, Matthew. Put the bird outside in the garden for ten minutes, and shut the door. I need to talk to you."

I closed the kitchen door, but I kept hold of Pox. In fact I probably kept hold of her a bit more than I should have because she fluttered a bit and I had to soften my grip so I didn't hurt her, but I was suddenly feeling vomity sick although I didn't know why. "Pox can't fly properly. A cat'll have her if I put her outside."

Mum started folding the cloth down into a perfect square. I don't reckon she'd heard me.

"I've been thinking about this since—well, since that 'upset' we had. Wondering what to do for the best. Wondering what's the right thing to say . . ." She started picking at the cloth and these tiny bits of blue fluff began drifting down. It made me think of Erin's dove trick. "There are things I need to tell you," she said.

"About me not being enough?"

"No. That's not how it was. But that is what I want to talk about."

"Go on then."

"It's a long story." She glanced at the clock, and I reckoned she was going to try and bottle out. "I've got to take Mark swimming when he gets in. Why don't we go through it when I get back."

I felt sort of flashed up. "So you reckon Mark's swimming is more important than stuff about me?"

"It's just . . ." She shook her head. "I want to do this properly. I want to explain it as carefully as I can."

"Do it now." I'd never been like that with her before. Never really pushed like that.

She was still shaking her head. "I want you to understand that I love you. That I don't regret you."

I remembered the last thing Kirsty had hit me with. "But I was weird. I wasn't turning out the way you and Dad wanted. Why don't you just spill it?"

"Because . . . that's not it. That's not what I'm trying to say."

"What then?"

"Matthew—I need you to understand—I was very young."

I didn't get what she was going on about. "So?"

She started pressing her hand against her lips, like she wanted to find a way to stop words coming out. And then she suddenly whispered, "You and Mark have different fathers."

There was this clanking great silence and when I finally managed to speak I wasn't even sure it was me making the sounds. "That's not true. You'd have told me." I didn't believe her. And anyway I'd have known. Of course I'd have known. Wouldn't I?

"I'm so sorry, Matthew."

My head filled up with Alex. What he'd looked like. How he'd been. But then I'd never been close to him. Never got on with him. And to tell you the truth I'd hardly even missed him after he went. That had got to me sometimes, the way I hadn't missed him. I used to think that I *should* miss him. I used to think you should miss your dad whatever crap sort of a person he'd been. I used to think it was part of what was wrong with me—the fact that I couldn't feel that "Dad" stuff about him. So maybe Mum was making sense. A messed-up, stuffed-up, miserable sense.

"Who then? Who was my dad?"

Her voice was really quiet and I had to lean forwards to hear her above the rain. "I met him through the church. I used to go there with Grandma to help, and he was someone who'd been in trouble. The vicar had found him a place to stay, and it all started with me taking things round there to help him move in."

I was stroking Pox's wings, as if I needed something to do with my hands. She'd gone quiet and still, like she knew this was a major blow up and she had to keep out of it.

"Nobody knew I'd fallen for him, and Grandma would have gone mad and put a stop to it. In fact, when I got pregnant with you, she did go mad."

I wasn't taking it in properly. It was like I was in someone else's skin, standing there listening to someone else's crapped-up life story. I sort of croaked out, "Why would she have gone mad? What was so terrible about him?" I wanted to know. I didn't want to know.

"He just . . . he wasn't quite balanced, I suppose. I think he ended up in prison in the end."

I couldn't speak. A nutter criminal. Weird weird weird.

"He was good-looking," she said suddenly,

like that was an excuse for him. Or maybe for her. "For a while I thought he was beautiful."

I didn't want to get my head round it. Mum and the nutter criminal. Who the hell was I? What the hell was I? Then this new idea hit me. "So my other dad—Alex—if I hadn't been around it would all have been different for you and him. He'd have still been here. You and him and Mark. All playing Happy Families together. You were right—it wasn't that I wasn't enough. You didn't want me at all. Or at least Alex didn't. I was in the effing way."

Mum looked like I'd stuck her in this cage and she couldn't find the door out. "You got more difficult when Mark came along, and neither Alex or I were coping."

"So sorry to have messed up your chances of a wonderful perfect family."

"I don't mean that."

My hands wouldn't stop shaking even with the warmth of Pox pressing against them. I was pretty close to throwing up. Like all this pain would come vomiting up out of me, sloshing down onto Mum's super-clean floor.

Mum put her hand out to touch my arm. "I didn't mean for things to happen with your dad. It . . . it just got out of hand."

I jerked back from her. "So I was an accident. Is that what you're telling me?"

"Just . . . try and understand. I want you to understand."

We were staring at each other. Her face was sort of wild, and I guess mine was too. I got this feeling like there was this huge hole in the centre of me and the wind was blowing through. And I did understand. It was all making sense. More sense than anything had ever done in my life.

"I always meant to tell you," she was whispering. "I just—I didn't want to make things any worse."

I pressed my head against the kitchen door, feeling the weight of the wood lean back as if it was trying to fight me. Then I got this idea that the whole house was trying to fight me. In fact I was pressed up against the whole effing world.

"Does he know about me? My dad. Does he know about me?" The whole of my life suddenly hung on her answer. If he didn't know, I would make it be all right. I would go and find him and discover he wasn't a nutter criminal. Mum just hadn't understood him. I could see how that would have happened. And we could build this amazing relationship. I'd seen telly programmes about stuff like that—kids turning up on their parents' doorsteps just out of the blue and every- thing. Everyone crying and life suddenly being great.

"Yes," she said. "He knew."

Effing nutter criminal. Of course he'd known.

She looked round as the front door clicked open and Mark came racing through from the hall. "I've got a swimming lesson in half an hour. We have to hurry."

"We might have to give it a miss today, dar- ling. We might—"

"Don't bother." I cut her off. "Don't let me stuff things up for you and Mark any*more*. And anyway, I'm going out."

Mark screwed up his face at me. "Why's Matthew got a pigeon?"

"Not now, darling." Mum hesitated, looking from him to me. "Maybe we both need a bit of time to calm down. We'll talk again when I get back. Things will be better, now that it's all out in the open."

She gave me this washed-out sort of smile and I got this picture in my head of her and the nutter criminal and the vomity pain rushed into my throat again. Mum switched this stupid expression onto her face like she was trying to calm down an old biddy who'd had her handbag nicked or something.

"Perhaps you could make a shoebox nest in the shed for the pigeon. Perhaps a pigeon isn't such a bad idea, after all."

"Sure." I shrugged. But I knew I wouldn't, because it suddenly didn't matter anymore. I'd made a decision. A big one. I was getting out. And I reckoned that, however much Mum tried to pretend she really wanted me, deep down she wouldn't give a stuff if I was gone.

As soon as she and Mark had driven off I hoicked out my old school sports bag from under my bed and settled Pox inside it, making a nest for her with spare jeans and boxers and stuff. I pushed the carved box thing that Erin had given me into my jacket pocket. I didn't want to leave it for Mum to chuck out when she couldn't flog it at the next jumble sale. Then I went back down to the kitchen.

That cash box was still in the drawer. I didn't take much. Even when I'm really hacked off I don't nick stuff unless it's things like those roses, which are going to grow again the next year anyway. And this was more of a loan. Once I'd got a job and saved a bit, I'd send it back. Maybe I'd send more. Maybe I'd end up rich and famous and send lorries full of dosh home for the rest of my life. Borrowing fifty quid wasn't such a bad thing when I thought about it like that. Maybe the son of a nutter criminal would turn out to be someone okay after all.

I rang Erin. I reckoned at least I should tell *her* I was going. "Can you meet me at the castle? I'll wait for you on the bridge." I wanted to go up there one last time, and I didn't want to tell her stuff over the phone.

"You sound terrible. Are you okay?"

"Yes. No. I just need to see you."

I zipped up the sports bag, turned Mark's alien-school picture round so it was facing the wall, and went back out through the rain.

And I reckon if Mum and Mark had passed me just then I'd have looked the other way, just the same as I did when I passed Billy coming back down the path from the castle.

I ran most of the way, keeping my head down to shield my eyes from the rain. When I got to the bottom of the hill I nearly collided with Billy. He scared me a bit because he looked wild and high, and ran off down Station Road. He didn't look at me but even if he had I don't think he'd have known who I was.

★

The handrail on the bridge was broken, so I didn't step up onto it. It looked pretty slippy and I got the bad feeling and the churning in my gut, so I didn't want to risk it. I saw Erin at the bottom of the hill and I got this rush of warmth knowing that she'd braved the weather just to come and see me. I reckoned she was my one real mate. Thinking like that made me get hold of her and hug her as soon as she reached me. "I've got something to tell you."

"Go on."

"I don't fit here."

"What d'you mean?"

"Everything's wrong. I'm a mess. An accident . . ." I held back from saying anything else. There was so much stuff she didn't know, and it would take too long.

"What are you going to do?"

"I'm picking up the next Waterloo train and I'll hang round somewhere like Covent Garden. I'll get a job. Sweeping. Washing up. Anything."

I could see she was pretty choked up with tears and I felt like a slimeball again. I'd started off being the Pied Piper and I'd ended up more like one of the rats.

"Don't tell anyone where I am," I said.

"I won't."

"You've been a good mate. I'll miss you." My voice came out gritty, but it wasn't the frog voice. It was more film hero stuff. I wished I could have sounded like that earlier, with Kirsty.

Erin was whispering something but what with the rain and the wind I could hardly hear her. Then she pressed her head into my shoulder and just stood against me, crying. It really got to me, her being so gutted. So I kissed her. Not a snog—not anything like I'd been going for with Kirsty—it was just a sort of thanks. "I've got to go. The train's due." I squeezed her once more, and went.

Matt was waiting by the bridge. As soon as he saw me he pulled me to him really tight, just holding on like he'd never let me go. I know it sounds cheesy, but I can remember thinking it was one of the most beautiful moments of my life. That whole row with Mum just floated away.

"I've got something to tell you." He sounded choked up, like everything inside him was churning.

"Go on." I squeezed my eyes shut.

"I don't fit in with anyone here."

"What d'you mean?"

"Everything's wrong. I'm a mess. An accident . . ." He stopped, as if he couldn't bring himself to say anything else.

I clung on to him as if he was driftwood in the sea and there was a huge wave coming. I wanted to tell him that he wasn't wrong with me. That as far as I was concerned he was right. Exactly right. But I was scared that he might not want to hear it. I was scared it might not be enough. So instead I said, "What are you going to do?"

"I'm picking up the next Waterloo train and I'll hang round somewhere like Covent Garden. I'll get a job. Sweeping. Washing up. Anything."

I clung on tighter. The wave had come. I was being swept away to somewhere bleak and barren.

"Don't tell anyone where I am."

"I won't."

I pressed my head into his chest. I could feel his heart thumping through his jacket.

"You've been a good mate," Matt whispered fiercely. "I'll miss you."

"I'll miss you too," I whispered back.

He squeezed me tighter. "I've got to go," he said at last. "The train's due."

And it was then that it happened. He kissed me. There were no teeth or noses. It was gentle. Beautifully wonderfully magically gentle. And then he was gone.

I followed this path that took me under a bridge and along the edge of the Thames. There were Christmas lights and music and stuff and it got to me because it wasn't even December yet.

Father Christmas was doing burgers by the railings. There were these benches set out along the walk, fancy ones between the lamp-posts. I sat down, trying to make out I was hooked on watching the rain ripple the river. Not that any-one was looking.

I put Pox on my shoulder and she perched there looking round like she was wondering what was going on. Her and me both.

It was early evening and I didn't know what the hell to do next. The rain turned to sleet. I kept thinking about Kirsty.

I like you. Lots.

How the hell had I got it so wrong? What had she been doing? What had she wanted? And the Dad stuff. I was still gutted about the

Dad stuff. Although I hadn't wanted Alex. And I didn't want the nutter criminal. It was just that I didn't know who the hell I was. And thinking like that scared me.

From the nearby subway someone was playing "Away in a Manger" on a violin. I reckoned it was the saddest sound I'd ever heard.

The music stopped and it grew colder. I'd move on in a second. My feet were icing over inside my trainers, and I wished Kirsty had at least given me back my scarf.

"That's so beautiful."

I looked round. This girl was standing watching me, swinging a violin case. She had short-cropped silvery hair that sort of glittered and glowed and I reckoned she looked like the closest thing to an angel I'd ever seen.

I thought she meant the Christmas decorations were beautiful—the reflection on the water or something, so I did this sort of grunt, "Yeah."

"Especially with the light spilling over you."

Spilling. *Spilling*. It really got me the way she said that. I reckoned it was like a poem. Not that I knew anything about poetry. I'd got left behind after "Humpty Dumpty," to tell you the truth.

She gave me this smile. "How did you get him

to do that?" And I realized that she wasn't going on about decorations dancing on water. She was talking about me. Or at least—not quite me— Pox.

"It's . . . he's a girl." Christ, what a geek. *He's a girl.* He's a girl. "I mean . . ."

She laughed. "I know what you mean." And she just kept standing there like she was waiting for me to say the next thing.

I couldn't come up with anything though. I'm not that great at talking to girls I don't know.

In the end I guess she got fed up waiting because she said, "Pigeons are special. People never notice them because there's too many of them, but I do. I love the colours." She looked at Pox. "Your bird is soft grey and mottled, but every one is different. That pigeon by the bin is pastel pink. You see it when it goes under the street lamp."

I nodded at the pastel-pink pigeon in a way that showed her I could see exactly what she meant. I even put Pox down on the ground for a second. I got this naff idea that they could be mates. Except the pastel-pink pigeon sort of huffed up and pecked at Pox, and Pox flapped and strutted behind my legs.

I put her back on my shoulder. "Bad idea."

The girl laughed. "My name's Sarah. What are you doing here?"

She had this soft voice. She looked good, too. I reckoned I might even have gone for her if I hadn't been so caught up with Kirsty. But anyway I was weird. An accident. A girl like her wouldn't stay round me for long.

"I'm . . ." I hesitated. I could tell her anything. I was never going to see her again. I didn't have to let on that I was this complete geek who didn't know what the hell he was playing at. My hand touched Erin's cards in my pocket. "I'm a magician. Sort of. Between jobs."

She smiled like she was someone who bumped into sort-of magicians every second of the day and night and said, "I believe in magic. I don't mean card tricks and sawing people in half. I mean real magic. I think the world's full of incredible things, but most people are too tuned out to realize."

"Yeah." I nodded, making out I knew exactly what she was on about, again, and searched round in my head for some sort of amazing reply.

Nothing came, but it was okay because she kept on talking. "I'm a performer too. I'm at music college." She tapped the side of her violin case. "Performing is a way of life, isn't it?"

"Yeah." I flicked a grin at her, like we were both in the same gang or something.

"Where are you staying?"

"I'm between places at the moment." I know it sounded naff but I suddenly wanted to keep her near me. I got this idea that all the time she was standing there I still existed.

"I'm sorry. I know loads of people our age who are like that. It's rough, isn't it?" She brushed the sleet out of her hair with her fingers. "You can't get a place to live if you haven't got a job, and you can't get a job if you haven't got a place to live."

I felt gutted, all that rich and famous sending dosh home stuff sliding away. I hadn't known all that about jobs and places to live. Or at least, I hadn't thought about it. I stared at the river again and there was a swirl of plastic cups and party streamers and this burst balloon floating by.

When I looked up again, Sarah was gone.

Pox shifted on my shoulder so I lifted her down and tucked her inside my jacket. I'd buy us both a burger to share.

As I walked over to Father Christmas my head got choked up with Kirsty again. And I got this idea then that maybe it was better never to expect anything, than to want stuff you can never have.

★

Time just stopped. That was how it felt, from the second I got back home. I was trapped in an endless lump of nothing and I couldn't find my way out of it.

Mum came into my room. "Can we talk?"

I stared out of the window, watching the street lamp pour its hazy light down onto the pavement. Maybe Matt would magically appear in the glow.

"Erin . . . I'm sorry. I shouldn't have gone at you like that."

Of course, Mum thought it was that row that had sent me off into this dazed trance. I wasn't going to tell her anything different. All those things she'd said earlier about Matt being a bad influence—she'd probably be glad he was gone. She put her hand on my shoulder. I flinched away.

"I'm just so worried about you. You've never been in trouble at school before."

He'd be in London by now. It would be scary, having to make his way through the streets on his own.

"We can work this out. But we need to talk some more about Dad."

"Are you getting back together?" I said this suddenly. Unexpectedly.

Mum sighed. "We're trying to understand exactly what went wrong. That's enough for the moment."

I picked Mum's mascara off the windowsill and made it disappear. With a flick of my wrist I brought it back again. "I don't get why you're making it so easy for Dad. If it was me, I'd slam the door in his face."

"Try not to judge him," Mum said quietly. "It wasn't all his fault. The twins' coming didn't help, but if I'm honest, things were difficult before that."

The mascara floated above my palm and I watched its ghosted reflection in the glass. Mum and Dad had had years and years to understand each other. If they hadn't got it right in all that time, I couldn't see that they ever would.

"We married too young. He was my first real boyfriend and then you came along and it all seemed so perfect. I still had my head full of dreams and I . . ."

I moved my palm away and the mascara dropped like sudden death onto the windowsill. I blocked my ears with my fists.

I suddenly didn't want to talk to Mum. I didn't want to listen. I didn't want to know. She touched my shoulder once more, and then went.

Nobody who hasn't spent a night on the streets knows how cold it gets. Or how long it lasts.

There were dossers huddled in shop doorways and between dustbins and cramped up in cardboard boxes. It really got to me, this world that people like my mum reckon they know something about but they don't. I kept walking through the sleet, making my legs take one step and then another. One step and then another. I even said it to myself. One step and then another. One step and then another. I was aching and cold and so pig-tired and I got this longing just to lie down and sleep.

All the doorways were taken but I passed one that seemed wider than the others. This mechanical nativity scene turned slowly round in the window display. A tinsel banner stretched just inside the door. SEASONS GREETINGS TO ALL OUR CUSTOMERS. I reckoned I could kip in the corner. There was another bloke but he was asleep and I was careful not to disturb him as I stepped across.

Except he wasn't asleep. He sprang up. I tried to duck away but he grabbed me, scrunching my jacket in his fists. "No room, mate."

"Sorry." I twisted sideways, worried about Pox getting knocked off my shoulder. One step and then another. One step and then another.

Outside, the sky sleeted down. Usually I love wild weather. Bruised black clouds and stinging rain and the way the trees twist in the wind. Tonight I could only think about Matt. It was hopeless, trying to sleep. Instead my thoughts lit two words that burned through me.

Please ring. Please ring. Please ring.

I tried to imagine where he might be. I thought about grey buildings and gutters and shadowed figures lurking. The night stretched on. I wished there really were such things as mind-reading and telepathy. I pictured my thoughts leaving my head and zooming off through the darkness. They would be neon bright, like the adverts that flashed down from the hoardings high above the London streets.

Please ring. Please ring. Please ring.

Across the landing the twins started to

cry. I heard Mum get up. The luminous yellow face of my alarm clock shone out 12:05 a.m. Hours and hours before the morning washed in. I didn't think I could bear it. I pulled on my dressing gown and rummaged under the bed for the stack of *Gossip* magazines.

"BYE BYE BABY—DON'T WASTE YOUR DAYS DREAMING ABOUT THE GUY WHO'S GONE. CUT LOOSE AND GET FREE."

I didn't want to think like that. I didn't want to read *Gossip* anymore. I ought to dump the whole lot in the bin.

Please ring. Please ring. Please ring.

And then the phone went. I raced down the stairs, but even before I'd snatched up the receiver, it had stopped. I tried 1471. A withheld number. It had to be him though. He'd try again.

"What are you doing down there?" Mum appeared at the top of the stairs with Lily in her arms.

"Somebody rang."

"Who was it?"

"I . . . they . . . it just went dead."

"A wrong number, I expect. No one we know would ring at this time of night. Go back to bed and try and get off to sleep, or you'll never be up for school in the morning."

I went slowly, climbing into bed and pulling the duvet up over my head. The shadowed figures were moving, skulking out from dark alleys and following him down the street. The neon messages zapped and flashed behind my eyes.

Please ring. Please ring. Please ring.

This all-night café appeared like a naff kind of vision. I tucked Pox back in the sports bag and went in. There were cardboard angels hanging from the ceiling and they all swayed about and bashed into each other as I pushed through the door.

"What d'you want?"

"Coffee. Please."

The woman served me without looking at me. She wore these dangly Christmas tree earrings that lit up every other second. I reckoned she was my mum's age. Mum. Mark. I didn't want to think about them.

It was good to be inside. I sat by a window that had been sprayed with this silver frost. A string of girls in tight short skirts and fast clipping heels went past. Sometimes cars slowed right down and drove beside them. Sometimes the girls got in. This fight broke out across the street. There was shouting and swearing and I heard glass breaking. I made that coffee last a long time.

"Anything else?" The woman started wiping the table next to me. I knew what she meant. She meant—if you're not having anything else, then go. But like I said she was around my mum's age and I reckoned she might even have teenage kids of her own, so I started to say, "Do you know any-where I could kip tonight?"

Her face sort-of closed up and she began scrubbing the table even harder. I got the idea. I'm not really someone who needs stuff spelt out to them. The angels swayed and banged into each other again as I left.

I had one more try—an all-night video shop stacked with the sort of films Mum would have had a seizure about had this hostel next to it. The window had bars all wound with gold tinsel. There was this buzzer outside and a sign saying PRESS FOR INFORMATION.

I pressed.

"Sorry, mate." A bloke's voice crackled through on the intercom. "You have to get here earlier. We fill up by dusk this time of year." I

156

could see the security guard through the window. I knew it was him who was talking but he didn't look out at me or anything. One foot and then another. One foot and then another.

The voices started muttering on like they were worried about something and I had to keep telling them to shut up. Then I got worried that I would look like I was talking to myself, like those nutters you see walking the streets. I wondered what Kirsty was doing. I wished I had her number. I'd have rung her, although I didn't know what the hell I'd say. But anyway I didn't have her number so I reckoned it would be good to call Erin instead. I even found a phone booth. I did 141 to block out the call in case her mum picked it up, and let it ring twice. Only then I got sight of Mark's old watch. Either it was duff, or it was just gone midnight. There was a good chance Erin would be asleep. I hung up and walked on.

"Come in." Mr. Macey was pacing his office. Mr. Macey. Pacey Macey.

He had a file open in his hand. "We're concerned about you." He skimmed through the papers. "You came to this school with good reports. Your last school says you were hard-working and conscientious."

Matt had *tried* to ring. So he was thinking of me. And he hadn't been mugged and beaten, left bruised and bloodied in a sleazy gutter.

"Is there anything worrying you? Anyone upsetting you?" Mr. Macey dropped the file onto his desk and stood with his hands behind his back.

I knew he meant Matt. Why wouldn't they leave him alone? My voice spat spikes and splinters. "No."

The rain smacked the window. From under a pile of papers, a phone beeped.

"I'm going to issue you with a progress card. Your teachers sign it after each lesson, and we'll review their comments at the end of the week." Mr. Macey unearthed his phone and held his finger poised over the button. "Where are you due next?"

"English."

"Just apologise to Mr. Nelson and walk a straight line from now on. Remember—your name will be linked with every waylaid watch. With every bend in the canteen cutlery. With any person or persons who have mysteriously disappeared."

I walked back down the corridor. That

kiss. Did it count as my first snog? Snog was such a horrible word—really ugly—a grubby sound for something so wonderful.

"Sorry," I mumbled to Mr. Nelson as I walked into the classroom.

"Sorry what?"

"Sorry. Sir."

Mr. Nelson rocked forwards. "If you hadn't written such a vivid viewpoint for Gregory you might not have got off so lightly. But you'll stay in at lunchtime all week and give me a viewpoint for five additional minor characters."

I sat at the back, by the window, and looked "snog" up in the school dictionary. Snog: to kiss and cuddle. So maybe it did count.

Mr. Nelson turned back to the class. "Now today I want us to discuss some of the constraints a poet puts on himself when he tries to make his work rhyme."

I scribbled on my organiser:

"I love Matt
And that is that."

Followed by

"If I make this poem rhyme
Matthew Mason will be mine."

Not exactly Shakespeare I know, but I had
been awake all night.

"Oh please come back.
I cannot bear
That I am here
While you are . . ."

The last word shrivelled on the end of my
pen as I followed the movement of heads that
turned towards the window. A police car slid
slowly through the puddles in the car park.
PC Barlow got out, slammed the door, and
strode towards the main reception. Panic
washed through me. He must have come
about Matt. He'd want to talk to anyone that
might have seen him recently. Pacey Macey's
last words rang a warning in my head: "Your
name will be linked with any person or persons who have mysteriously disappeared."

Would they link Matt with me?

"The day was drenched
with questions

For those who knew you well.
But only I had the answers.
And magicians never tell."

I was knackered. My legs were doing me in and my trainers had rubbed these killer blisters on to my heels. I started thinking about sitting down. It made me want to cry, to tell you the truth. Just the idea of it.

The sky was getting light and I reckoned the tubes might be starting up. I could ride between stations for a bit. I bought a ticket at Leicester Square but the barrier jammed the second I tried to get through. It cheesed me off. Even when I was a kid barriers had always jammed up on me. Then this bloke in a uniform started walking towards me, and suddenly sitting on a train didn't seem like the best plan. I went up the steps and back out into the street.

Most places were still shut, but the dossers were waking up. They were stacking cardboard boxes outside the shops. One old bloke was folding his blanket. He smoothed it into a neat edged square like it was about to go into the airing cupboard or something. It really got to me, seeing him do that. I stopped and gave him some dosh even though he wasn't begging or anything. "Take care, mate." I sort of patted him, which was naff but I wanted to reach him somehow and I didn't know how the hell to do it. He touched his arm where my hand had been and I could feel him watching me walk away. I felt pretty down about the whole thing, to tell you the truth. It wasn't enough just to go round patting people and chucking them dosh and thinking you were making everything okay.

It was then that I saw this sign to Covent Garden. It was where I'd told Erin I'd be and I reckoned it was as good a place to go as anywhere, so I went. As I walked towards it, I could see it was already heaving with traders setting up stalls and stuff. A few people looked at me and smiled but I could tell it was mainly because of Pox. She was still on my shoulder, just perched up there like she was enjoying the ride.

A gang—my sort of age—were leaning against a wall with instruments and microphones and battered-up boxes. I wanted to talk to them. I don't know why. They just looked like they wouldn't mind.

"You all performers?" Stupid question, but I didn't know what else to start with.

"We hope." A girl who was sprayed silver got this knife out of her pocket and stuck it down her throat.

"Christ." I did a thing with my eyebrows to let her see how blown away I was. "How d'you do that?"

"I could teach you."

"I'll give it a miss today, thanks." I reckoned that was pretty sharp of me, off the cuff and everything. Witty. Amazing.

She laughed and her teeth were yellow against the silver. "I like the pigeon. Nice touch. Have you got an act?"

I wished I had. It would be good to have an act. And good to hang around with a gang like hers. I nearly got the cards out but it seemed pretty naff next to knife swallowing.

"Only you need a licence here," she went on. "You can't just turn up. If you go round the corner, by the transport museum, it's free."

"Okay." I nodded like she'd told me something I needed to know.

She turned away and started sharpening a silver sword.

As I walked off I saw this church.

There were people about, going down the path like it was the sort of place anyone could turn up at. I reckoned it would be okay to go in for a bit. There are seats in churches.

MY HOUSE SHALL BE A HOUSE OF PRAYER FOR ALL PEOPLE.

That was what it said inside the door.

There was this choir singing "Silent Night" and candles everywhere. I liked the candles. They looked sort of comforting so I sat near them and the way they were flickering about made that crying stuff want to start up again. I nearly did too. I had to stare round at the walls and try and think about something else just to stop tears streaming out and running all over my face. I got this idea that if I started crying I might never stop.

There was all this writing—memorials—on the walls. Gracie Fields. Charlie Chaplin. Anna Neagle. I'd heard of them, although apart from Charlie Chaplin I hadn't got a clue who they were.

There were these candelabras hanging from the ceiling. Behind them were two arched stained-glass windows. The sun was coming through—spilling through—onto the stone wall. I wanted to go nearer so I stood up and walked over, softly softly. I always walk like that when I'm in a church. When I got close to the windows I held my hand towards the reflection and the

164

colour spilled across me, too. It was weird but I felt sort of lifted, just looking at it. Like the world was really an all right place and everything would be okay in the end.

This sudden noise got me all jittery for a second, like a flock of something was rushing past. And then I realised it was only clapping outside. The silver girl must have started gulping down her knives.

There was this painting hanging between the windows. It was Jesus holding his hands up and angels flying round bringing him crowns and crosses. I got this idea he was holding his hands up to ask them to stop. You know like "Hey, guys. Give me a break. That's enough."

I reckoned he'd probably got boxes up in Heaven crammed full of crowns and crosses. A bit like our garage with all Mum's jumble.

I thought about Mum and Mark again. I ought to send them a message. A postcard or something. It would be the right thing. Being in a church does that to you, I guess. Even if you don't believe in it, it still makes you want to do the right thing.

I was even sorry about turning Mark's picture round. It wasn't his fault about Alex and the nutter criminal dad who I didn't want to think about. And Mark wasn't any better off than me. Alex had legged it too. I started thinking about Erin's dad and Kirsty's dad and then I got this idea that maybe dads weren't so great after all anyway. Who the hell would want one?

Apart from Jesus perhaps. His dad was supposed to be okay.

I looked at that "Hey, guys" Jesus for ages and ages and I might have stayed looking at him for longer except this vicar bloke appeared. I wouldn't have minded talking to him except he said it wasn't okay to have a pigeon in the church because she might crap on the floor. Except he didn't say "crap." He said "do something unpleasant."

I reckoned it was a bit off that he was kicking me out because of Pox. From what I remembered Jesus liked animals and birds and stuff. But I left anyway. It didn't seem like the sort of thing worth having a row about.

The police car splashed through a puddle as it cruised past, spraying my jacket with water.

"I bet they're looking for Kirsty Carter. She never went home last night." Tom switched sides with me and brought his umbrella down lower over our heads.

"How d'you know?" I watched the car swish away round the corner and felt the panic drain out of me. PC Barlow hadn't been looking for Matt after all.

"Billy Owen got called into Macey's office. Everyone in our tutor group was going on about it."

"Does Billy know where she is?"

"They said not, but he's out of his head half the time. He's getting really bad. He probably forgets his own name some days."

"I'd hate that. What d'you think makes him do it?"

Tom shrugged. "His mum and dad chuck money at him, but they're not around much to see what he wastes it on."

"Do you know him outside school then?"

"My mum does his mum's ironing. They live in that big white house up the road from the station. The one with the pillars by the front door."

"And what about Kirsty? She takes drugs too, but I've seen her mum's car and they can't have loads of money."

"Billy pays for everything. He likes controlling people. Especially her."

"Why?" I'd never thought about people

controlling other people before. Tom was sounding as if he was about a million years old.

"Kirsty's a tease. She flirts with anything in trousers."

I stepped outside the umbrella to dodge a puddle and then stepped back under again. "Has she done that with you then?"

Tom walked straight through the middle of the puddle and glanced sideways at me. "No. I'm probably the only bloke in our year she hasn't tried it on with, though."

"You don't like her?" I was puzzled. I would have thought someone like Tom would have seen Kirsty as a distant star. Misty and mysterious and hopelessly unattainable.

"I'd rather have someone I could trust."

The wind wrestled the umbrella, punching it inside out. I waited while he sorted it, thinking about Matt. Tom was right. Even older than a million years. You'd live life walking barefoot across broken glass if you were with someone you couldn't trust.

And then, holding the umbrella over me again, Tom said, "I'd trust you."

"I . . . thank you." My voice had a shocked piglet sort of squeak. Please don't let him mean what I thought he meant.

But he did mean what I thought he meant, and he must have thought the shocked piglet squeak meant I meant it too, because he put his arm round me and pulled me closer.

I moved away. Almost jumped. "I really like you." Squeak squeak. Nervous giggle. "But it's—well, I think of you as a friend."

He stopped walking, dropping the umbrella down as if he'd forgotten he was holding it. "You think I'm a geek."

"It's not that." I tried to make it sound as if I would fancy him if things were different. "But . . . I'm going out with someone else."

The rain lashed us. It washed into Tom's eyes and he brushed it away. I stared down at my shoes. I was so so sorry.

He started walking again, reaching for my arm and pulling me back under the umbrella. "Who?"

"I can't tell you."

"Is he married or something?"

I did the nervous giggle again, although I didn't think the idea of married blokes and young girls was particularly funny. "It's nothing like that. We just . . . we haven't really told anyone yet. And my mum doesn't like us being together."

"Romeo and Juliet eat your hearts out."
His voice was steamrollered. How would I
have felt if Matt had said anything like that
to me?

Reaching Tom's gate we stood awkwardly
as the rain drummed a dead beat over our
heads. He handed me the umbrella. "You
keep this. Give it back once the ark is ready."
Oh, Tom. Tom. Still joking. Still friendly.
Still looking after me. I suddenly put my
hand up and touched his cheek.

"You're sweet," I whispered.

He gripped my fingers roughly over the
handle and it surprised me how strong he
was. Then he turned and walked quickly up
his path to his front door.

I spent the next day moving between cafés, trying
to keep out of the rain. I reckon I must have
looked like a cup of coffee.

I passed this shop selling postcards, bought
one for Mum, and wrote "Everything's fine.
Getting sorted."—and then decided Mum
wouldn't give a stuff how I was so I stuck it in
a bin instead. And anyway it wasn't true. I
wasn't fine or sorted.

My trainers were rubbing more killer blisters

on the backs of my feet. I was wetter than a drowned frog. And the fifty quid was frittering away.

I knew I should try and find that shelter again. Put my name down or whatever it was you were supposed to do. But I didn't go looking for it. I'm like that about some things. Even when I know I should do something that's really important, I don't.

I came to this café that had "Happy Snacks" done in scratched yellow across the window. I put Pox back in the bag and pushed through the door. A worn-looking bloke nodded at me from behind the counter. "Still raining?"

It gets me when people say stuff like that. I wanted to tell him I'd been swimming in the Thames, but I managed to stop myself. "Just a bit."

"What would you like?"

"Coffee."

I looked round as his machine frothed the white foam out into a cup. There were no decorations anywhere. No signs of Christmas. On the wall behind him there was this pair of kids' pink ballet shoes hung over a picture of Jesus nailed on the cross. Next to that there was this blackboard with a chalked-up menu on it.

TODAY'S SPECIAL. SHEPHERDS' PIE.

"And a shepherds' pie," I added.

"One special, Annie."

I realised then that there was a woman in the corner, sitting beside a wheelchair with a kid in it.

Annie went off out the back and I sat down at one of the tables, thinking I wouldn't stare at the kid because staring at kids in wheelchairs is rude.

"Where you from?" The bloke brought the coffee over.

"Bournemouth." I don't know why I said that. I've never been to Bournemouth in my life, but the idea of it just sort of lit up in my head.

"We had a chip shop there once." Annie came out with my shepherds' pie on a tray and it struck me that she looked more washed-out than the bloke.

I didn't say anything. I didn't reckon there was anything to say. She went back to sit with the kid, and the bloke shuffled off behind the counter again.

Have you ever watched a stray dog eat? The way they just gulp and gulp without the food even touching the sides of their mouths. That was me with that shepherds' pie. Stuffing my face like a stray dog.

This scuffling started coming from my bag. Pox. I reckoned she could do with a few bits of potato or something, and glanced towards the bloke. He was chopping onions and the smell must have been getting to him because he kept wiping his eyes with the back of his hand. He wasn't looking at me so I pulled the zip open just a touch thinking I could feed Pox without him seeing, only she stuck her head out and made that pigeony thrumming noise. I tried to cover it with a cough but the woman was pretty sharp for someone who looked so washed away.

"What have you got there?"

I was going to bluff it and make out it was a toy or something but Pox had different ideas. She stuck her head right out and started looking round like she was wondering where her mashed potato had got to. "It's a pigeon," I said.

"What are you doing carrying a pigeon around?"

I remembered what I'd told Sarah. "I'm a sort of magician." The lie was easier second time round, like my mouth had got used to saying it. In fact I felt pretty laid back as I pulled Erin's cards from my jacket pocket. "She's part of my act."

The bloke stopped chopping onions and came

over with a handful of breakfast cereal, sprinkling it on the floor. "Where do you perform?"

"Covent Garden." That was easy too, like I'd been hanging out there all my life.

"They have some good acts." He crouched down to click his fingers at Pox.

I pulled the zip right open and lifted her onto the floor. She stabbed at the cereal a few times and then fluttered up to my knee, so I lifted her onto my shoulder.

The bloke straightened and put his finger out to touch her. "I shouldn't let you in here with her, but we used to breed birds. Doves mainly. You've got a good bond with this one, the way she trusts you. My daughter used to love letting . . ." He stopped talking, his onion juice eyes streaming again.

"What happened to your doves?"

"We had to get rid of them when we left Bournemouth. There's nowhere to keep them up here."

His voice had gone flat and I felt pretty down for him, to tell you the truth.

At the back of the café the kid started to cry. That got me down too. I wanted to cheer everyone up. "You need a bit of magic around," I told him. I remembered what Erin had said about putting on an act—making people believe you could do miracles and stuff, so I leaned back in my seat and gave the bloke this long look like I was seeing inside his mind. "Pick a card."

He pulled a card from the deck.

"Now put it back. Anywhere you like."

He stuck it in the middle.

"Okay. Now watch closely. I'm going to make your card jump to the top." I turned the first card over. It was the nine of hearts, which was the wrong card, but I'd done it on purpose. Erin had said it was a good tactic, especially for anyone who was a beginner. It was a way to practise covering up mistakes, so that when you really made one it wouldn't show. So my plan was to string him along a bit—make him wonder whether I was any good or not—and play for time. I made my voice sound hacked off. "That's not it, is it?"

"No." He sounded pretty hacked off too.

"Give me a bit of time. I need to try and tune into you a bit more." I burned another "I can read your thoughts" look at him, then said slowly, "I've got an idea growing in my head that your card was actually black."

"That's right."

Annie came over, the kid on her hip. The kid stopped grizzling and I got a look at her face.

Then I wished I hadn't. She was just staring at nothing with these blanked-out eyes. Sort of "the lights are on but there's nobody home" if you get what I mean.

"You must be special," said Annie. "Ella usually cries all the time when she's awake. She must like you."

I nodded but I didn't answer. I didn't reckon Ella would know the difference between a saint and a sausage, to tell you the truth.

I turned back to the bloke, "It's not a high number either, is it?" I shook my head suddenly, and opened my hand to him like I was giving up. "You're going to have to tell me."

"The four of clubs."

"Okay. I made a mess of it. These things don't work every time. Look—let's tear this nine of hearts up. I reckon it's getting in the way."

I made this big show of tearing it, holding it high for him and Annie to see. I was feeling okay. I knew I was awkward and not slick like Erin or anything, but she'd shown me the whole routine several times and I was pretty confident it was going to work. And from the way they were watching me I could tell they were buying into it all. It was as if they wanted to believe it. They wanted me to be really magic.

I pressed the torn-up pieces into the bloke's hand and turned up the top card again. "Hey, that's weird." I put this sort of tremble into my voice this time, like I couldn't quite get what was going on.

The bloke kept staring at me, the torn-up card still clutched in his fist.

I stared back. "I think I'm getting something now. Squeeze your fingers together. As tight as you can. Can you feel anything happening?"

He glanced at Annie and shook his head. Annie moved closer.

"Open your hand up. Maybe I've blown it again."

He opened his hand and Annie gave this sort of shriek, stepping back so fast the kid's head jerked and rolled.

The four of clubs was lying, in one piece, on the flat of the bloke's hand.

"I don't get it," Annie started saying. "Where's the torn-up nine?"

I flicked over the top card and held it up to her.

She was shaking her head. "You didn't even touch him. How . . ." She crossed herself and came really close to me.

The kid was grizzling again and I jolted for a second, not because of the grizzle but because I got this idea that there was this light hovering round her. I looked over to Annie and said, sticking the cards back in my pocket, "Ella's going to be okay." I wished straight away that I hadn't said it, but it just came out. If I'd thought about it I'd have known it was a crap thing to say.

Annie started gazing at me and there was this weird sort of buzzed-up look in her eyes, like she was really excited. "Don't go yet. I want to talk to you more."

I knew I'd gone too far and being in that café suddenly didn't seem such a good idea so I dropped a tenner on the table and picked up my bag. I wasn't even bothered about the change.

"Please stay. You've been sent, I know you have." Annie had hold of my arm and she was gripping me tight. It didn't hurt me or anything but I'm never that keen on being gripped tight by people who don't want me to leave. I had to think of something quick.

"I've got an act later. I can't miss it."

I nodded at them all, turned round, and legged it.

The castle was a grey ghost in the sleety afternoon. Leaning on the windowsill I tried to fill in the gaps of what it could have been like hundreds of years before. It was hard to imagine people actually living there. Working. Playing. Loving. Hating. Where did all the past go?

Mum was out at some sort of baby clinic, and the house was horribly quiet. I turned away from the window and flicked through the newest copy of *Gossip*—hunting out the latest pearls from Mystic Melissa. Mine was "NEW REVELATIONS TAKE A STRANGE TWIST THIS WEEK" and Matt's was "OLD LOVES DIE HARD."

Horoscopes were such a load of rubbish. And anyway, I wasn't really an old love. We'd only just begun.

A car drew up and stopped outside. A minute later there was a knock on the door. I hoped it wasn't Dad. I wasn't in the right mood for facing him. Perhaps I could just tell him I had masses of homework, and he'd go away again.

I dropped *Gossip* back down on the bed and hurried downstairs.

For a moment the woman startled me, standing under a peachy umbrella with a matching coat. Then I realised. It was Matt's mum.

"Erin. I'm sorry to call unexpectedly,

but I didn't want to ring. I wanted to speak to you in person. You know Matthew's gone?"

"No." The lie slithered out. "I haven't seen him for a couple of days."

"He took some money. No note. I'm so worried."

It lurched inside me—his mum being worried. I'd never thought about how she'd be taking it. "Mum's out, but I'll make you a cup of tea. Shall I take your coat?"

"I mustn't stay long. I've left Mark. He's terribly upset and he's staying off school." She shook the drips from her umbrella, propped it against the porch, and then followed me through to the kitchen. "The police were over until late last night. They asked lots of questions. I've got the most terrible headache."

"I don't know anything about where Matt is." I switched on the kettle and kept my back to her. It was all sounding grown-up and serious with everyone worried and panicking and asking questions. Matt running away belonged to the real world suddenly. Not a shrouded locked-away secret between him and me.

"They're concerned about the link

between Matthew and this girl who's disappeared from home."

Something in me jolted. "Kirsty Carter?
Why?"

"They both went missing yesterday. And I
know he's spent some time talking to you, so
I wondered if he'd ever spoken to you about
Kirsty."

Spent some time. Spent some time. It
sounded so casual. As if I could have been
anyone. Or no one. "Not really. I mean, he
knew Kirsty, but not very well."

"Matthew's been getting himself into
trouble ever since he could walk. He just
attracts it like a magnet." She twisted her
fingers together. I noticed they were long.
Bone thin. Like Matt's. "It's usually minor
incidents, but—well—they've all added up
and he's got a bad name for himself with the
police."

I dropped a tea bag into a mug and
poured on the boiling water. "He's always
lovely to me."

I felt warm when I said that. I had the best
of him. I knew the best of him.

She stopped twisting her fingers and
splayed them on the table. Peach fingernails.

I wondered if she'd done them before the police, or after. "You know, no one's ever had much of a good word for Matthew all his life. Not even me. I didn't mean to be hard on him but it was always so difficult and I so badly wanted him to—" She paused and stared down at the peach perfect nails. "—to be normal. And I've let him down. More than you might think. More than I can explain."

Something in her voice caught at me and I wanted her to keep talking but I was scared that if I said too much I might give Matt away, so I said, "I don't know where he is, but I can't see why he'd be with Kirsty." I handed her the tea. "They weren't even friends as far as I know."

I tagged on "as far as I know" to make it thin and light. Nothing to me one way or the other. Matt's mum sipped her tea. "Thank you for telling me that. The police seem—well, they're very insistent. I wouldn't want to cover up for Matthew if he was in proper trouble, but I don't want to have to think terrible things about him."

I couldn't work out what she meant. How could him going off with Kirsty make her think terrible things? But it didn't matter anyway because I knew he wasn't with her. My neon thoughts zapped out to find Matt. What would I do if he rang now, while his mum was still here? I glanced at her as she sipped her tea, and suddenly I wanted her gone.

She looked up and my feelings must have been written all over my face, because she said, "I have to go. I'm sure you've got things to do."

I got up to see her out. The rain squalled in on us as I opened the front door. "I'm sorry I can't help," I said.

"You have helped." She looked lost suddenly. "The police are hardly doing anything to look for Matthew because they say he's not a 'high risk' runaway. They seem to think he'll be coping. Ridiculous, isn't it? He can't even boil an egg on his own. It was always impossible to teach him anything."

I thought about all the magic I'd been showing him. "He might learn quicker than you think."

"You've got such a positive view of him." She ran her hand across her forehead. "I wish I'd seen him differently. We just—we don't know who anyone is really, do we? Not even the people we should love the most."

She snapped open the peachy umbrella and hurried back down the path to her car. I watched her drive away. I hadn't liked her much at first, but maybe I'd got her wrong. Maybe she was right about not knowing who anyone really is.

The rain stopped for a bit and some time about four o'clock I found myself back at Covent Garden. The knife-swallowing girl had gone and a clown was riding about on a unicycle. I'm not that keen on clowns, to tell you the truth. When I was a kid they always scared the hell out of me.

A woman with a barrow loaded with holly and ivy nudged my elbow. "Bunch of mistletoe, darling? Get lucky with someone tonight."

I shook my head.

"Come on. Nice-lookin' boy like you. Must be some girl you fancy your chances with."

What was Kirsty doing? What was she thinking? I got this idea about ringing Erin again, to ask her to check that Kirsty was okay. I'd have to give Erin a reason though. Or maybe I could tell her the truth about how I felt. I reckoned I could trust Erin with the truth.

"How many do you want?" The woman was holding up bunches for me to choose from.

I was about to say no again but her hair was as wet as mine and I suddenly got this picture in my head that she wasn't going home to anything good, so I stuck my hand in my pocket. "That one." I took it and handed her a fiver and waited for a minute but she didn't give me any change.

Two minutes later I gave the mistletoe to this girl who looked like she didn't get many bunches of mistletoe handed to her by strangers, if you get what I mean.

I walked up the outside of the square heading towards these Christmas lights that were lit up around the transport museum. A bloke with a ponytail—my sort of age—was standing outside, juggling fire-sticks. He was good. Amazing. But most people were just hurrying past loaded down with parcels and stuff and hardly anyone was watching.

There was a bench by a stall selling roasted chestnuts, so I sat down on it even though it was wet, just to give him a bit of an audience. I clapped every now and then and even chucked dosh in his hat. He grinned at me. He didn't seem too bothered that no one was taking any notice. It was like he was having an okay time anyway. It made me feel okay too, just watching him.

Somewhere nearby a brass band started belting out "Oh, Come All Ye Faithful." My foot began tapping inside my trainer, although it was pretty squelchy because of all the rain. Then I got Erin's cards out and started shuffling through them a bit, just as a way of keeping my fingers from freezing up.

The fire juggler was going for this grand finale where he was holding the flames inside his mouth. I reckoned he'd only have to breathe in and he'd be dead. I chucked him another quid. There was a bit of a crowd now but he hadn't earned much. It struck me that he was standing there, juggling with his life, and it was hardly worth anything to anyone.

It started drizzling again. Why the hell hadn't I gone to find that shelter?

"Praise God. I've found you. I've been looking all afternoon." I felt someone grab my arm from the side.

For a second I just froze. Mum! And then I got this relief flooding over me that whatever kind of stick she gave me and whatever muck was going on between us, there might be worse things than being back home again. I put Erin's cards down and stood up to face her, only then I saw that it wasn't Mum. It was that Annie woman from Happy Snacks.

"I could see that you had something . . ."

I started shaking my head. "I never touched a thing. I just stayed in that one seat. How could I have—?" I stopped. She didn't look like she was about to call the police and have me locked up and the key flushed down the loo.

She seemed sort of hyped up. "Please. We've moved here so we can be closer to Great Ormond Street Hospital but they haven't been able to do anything for Ella. Come back with me now. Do what you can."

Annie's eyes were locked on to me like they were burning into my brain. To tell you the truth, it was pretty scary. I reckoned she'd really lost it.

People were staring and she started calling stuff out to them. "Two years ago my little girl Ella went to the dentist to have a tooth out, but she didn't come out of the anaesthetic properly. She's been semi-comatose ever since. The doctors have been trying new drugs, but I'm losing hope. I've prayed every day for a miracle, and now . . ."

She was gripping my arm again. I was sorry

for Ella but I reckoned anything I said would make Annie worse. The fire juggler seemed to have given up and I got this idea that I'd ruined his act, and I didn't feel too great about that either.

"You've been sent to save her. I know you have. Please . . . don't let us down." She looked round at the crowd that was gathering. "He's got the Power. Believe me."

I'd had enough then. I legged it.

I weaved behind the fire juggler and turned the corner by the museum, breaking into a run. I'm not that great at running, to tell you the truth. I used to get a stitch every year on sports day, and kids like Billy Owen would be getting their winners' medals while I was still staggering across the finish line. I kept going for as long as I could but soon the pain in my side started doing me in and my breath was rasping in my throat and those killer blisters seemed like they were out to finish me off. I stopped running, leaning against this warehouse wall.

It was then that I felt another hand touch my arm.

It was early evening when the door knocker hammered.

"Erin Jones? My name is PC Barlow. I need to have a few words. Is your mum around?"

"She's upstairs, bathing my sisters."

I'd never spoken to a policeman on the doorstep before. Big feet. Big body. Big face. He could ask me anything. He could make me say anything.

"I'm sorry if this is inconvenient, but it's important, and I need an adult to be present."

Five minutes later we were all in the front room. Mum had the twins swaddled in fluffy white towels and their round saucer eyes stared out at PC Barlow as if he'd just touched down from another planet.

He took out a small tape recorder. "It's about Matthew Mason. His mother has told us he's a friend of yours."

"I don't know where he is."

"This isn't just about Matthew. We're linking him with the disappearance of a local schoolgirl. Kirsty Carter. How well do you know Matthew?"

"He's been here a few times. I do a bit of magic and I've been showing him some tricks."

"And how well do you know Kirsty Carter?"

This was easier. Safer. "She's in my year at school. We're not friends or anything."

"So you don't know anything about her relationship with Matthew?"

"She hasn't got a relationship with Matt. She goes out with Billy."

"Erin. This may be a serious enquiry. It's important for you to tell us everything you know."

"I am. Matt doesn't know Kirsty any more than he knows anyone else. She's just part of the gang that goes up to the castle."

"Billy Owen tells me a different story. He says Matthew is always hanging around Kirsty."

"You can't trust Billy with anything." I wanted to add about the drugs but I changed my mind. Best not to say too much. That way I wouldn't make any mistakes.

"So Matthew has never said anything about Kirsty to you. Never indicated an . . . er . . . an interest?"

My mind shuffled back to a few weeks ago, when he'd asked about her being in my year. It was nothing. Just an excuse to get me talking. And a million times too complicated to explain. "No."

Lucy squirmed suddenly and fidgeted in her fluffy white towel. A bottom smell soaked into the room. She began to squawk. Lily sucked her knuckle and stared at Lucy as if she had just learnt something terrible and world shattering. Then she started squawking too.

"I'm afraid . . . ," Mum began.

PC Barlow turned off his tape. "We may need to talk to Erin again."

I didn't say anything. Didn't look at him. Didn't show him to the door.

The day was drenched
With questions
For those who knew you well.
But only I had the answers.
And magicians never tell.

It was the fire juggler.

"You okay, mate?"

I just stared at him. To tell you the truth, I wasn't that used to having anyone call me "mate." Especially not with "You okay?" in front of it.

"Yeah." I straightened up, trying not to wince like a nerd.

"You forgot these cards. Left them on the bench." He handed me Erin's deck. "What was going on back there?"

"That woman just came at me. I'm a sort of magician and I did a trick in her café earlier. She came looking for me."

"What for?"

I shrugged. "Don't know. Just bonkers." I didn't want to go into it with him. I was still feeling pretty uncomfortable about all that miracle stuff, to tell you the truth. I should've kept my mouth shut when I'd seen that light round Ella earlier. I'd just caused a stack of trouble again now.

I didn't want to think about it and I reckoned the fire juggler must be more than a bit hacked-off with me, nicking his grand finale and everything, so I said, "It was amazing, that fire stuff you were doing."

"I thought you were waiting to go on after me, but we've got a queuing system. That's what I wanted to tell you. Why I followed you. We look out for each other round here, mate."

"Right." I felt good when he said that. The whole thing of being looked out for. I got the idea again about wishing I could perform. Do something decent that would make people want to hang around and watch. I wished I'd got more from Erin. I'd learnt some good stuff from her, but I hadn't done enough. I'm always like that, wishing things when it's too late to do anything about it.

The fire juggler started walking. He went at it like the whole thing was a walking race or something. It was hard to keep up, especially with the killer blisters.

"My name's Danny. What's yours?"

"Matt Mason. I've just come up from a place called Leigh Cove." Which wasn't that bright, seeing that I'd just done a runner and everything.

"So where d'you pick the pigeon up, mate?"

"She came from Leigh Cove too. She used to live at the castle but this bloke started giving her a hard time." I stopped talking then. I didn't want to move into hard-time conversations. I didn't want him to ask any hard-time questions about me.

The pavements got more uneven and there were puddles and rubbish and some bloke with a billboard round his neck spouting off about the end of the world. I got sprayed again and again by passing cars but I wasn't too bothered, to tell you the truth. I was pretty soaked anyway.

I wondered where the hell we were going,

though. Or whether Danny even wanted me with him. Maybe he was walking so fast because he was trying to shake me off. We passed this pub called The Lamb.

"Fancy a beer, mate? I made a few quid back there today." He grinned suddenly and I saw that he had half his front tooth missing. "Until you came along."

I don't drink much. The crowd at the castle were always getting out of it on lager or cheap cider and then throwing it all back up. I couldn't see the point. But Danny was calling me "mate" and it was raining pretty hard again. Having a pint didn't seem like the worst idea I'd ever heard, so I tucked Pox inside the sports bag and we pushed our way up to the bar.

The pub was done up like the landlord got a discount on bulk-buy Christmas decorations, if you get what I mean. And there was this tree in the corner that really got to me. It was leaning over and squashed on one side and the tinsel looked like it was about fifty thousand years old, but there was the smell of pine and a stack of parcels round the bottom and I suddenly felt sort of empty inside.

Danny nodded at this reindeer who was serving drinks. "Hi, sweetheart." He had to shout because of all the noise and the jukebox and everything, but she came straight over. I reckoned she looked young to be serving.

"How did it go today?" she said.

"Okay." Danny grinned. "Made enough for two beers anyway."

She glanced at me, then back at him again. "We're supposed to be saving what we earn."

"It's nearly Christmas."

She gave him one of those looks that girls can do sometimes, and began to pull the pints.

Danny turned to me. "Where you staying tonight?"

"Just about."

"Yeah. I've stayed in that hotel before too. The roof leaks and the food's crap."

He looked at me for a second longer while the reindeer slid our beers across the bar. Danny leaned forwards and said something to her. She looked worried for a moment, but then she smiled at him. She looked pretty okay when she smiled, even with that stupid reindeer head. "Jordan will like that. I'm picking him up from nursery when I finish here. I've got some business though."

She paused and lowered her voice so I couldn't make out the next bit, but Danny jerked back from her like she'd said something he didn't want to hear. She touched his face with the side of her hand and they stood for a minute, just looking at each other. They reminded me of Billy and Kirsty so I picked the pint up and knocked it back like it was orange squash on sports day. Then I stuck my hand in my pocket, thinking I'd get in a couple more beers to return the compliment, but all I had left was this twenty pence piece.

"I've got a place you can stay." Danny was back with me. "It's nothing great but it'll keep you dry. And safe."

"Sounds good." I didn't mention the dosh problem, but my head was feeling pretty light and I reckon I would have said yes to anything.

"I'll finish this, then we'd better get off." He emptied his glass. "I'll need to check in with a few people so they know who you are."

"Is it a hotel or something?"

He stared at me for a moment, and then gave me that broken-toothed grin. "You'll see, mate."

The reindeer was leaning over the other side of the bar while a bloke in a shabby suit whispered something in her ear. He looked pretty ugly, to tell you the truth. He had one of those mashed-up sort of noses and I reckoned it might be a good idea if he went on a diet for New Year, if you get what I mean. I thought the reindeer seemed okay about him though, because she giggled. Only then I saw her glance towards Danny. The giggle hadn't reached her eyes.

Danny looked pretty sick and turned away.

"White Christmas" kicked in on the jukebox as I followed him to the door. My head had gone a bit fuzzy. I was grinning, my smile stretching across my face, which probably made me more bonkers than Annie, given my circumstances. Then I banged into a table, spilling this bloke's drink. The bloke looked at me as if he didn't wish me anything merry or bright, but when I stopped to try and sort it out with him he didn't look too happy about that either.

Danny grabbed hold of my elbow and steered me back out into the street. The cold air caught my lungs and cut through the fuzzy stuff. I started seeing dossers and drunks and heard sirens nearby. Suddenly nothing felt funny any-more. So at least I knew I wasn't bonkers.

Dad was round again. "I've brought you something," he said.

I wanted to say that I didn't want any-thing from him, but I was still thinking about Tom. I remembered his eyes and the rain running down his face and I felt horrible.

"So You've Played a Part in Breaking His Heart."

"Erin, sweetheart—I said I've brought you something."

"What is it?"

He handed me an envelope and I opened it slowly. "Membership of the Young Magicians Club?" I held up the card. "This is from the Magic Circle."

"I've been finding out about it for you. You'll get a monthly magazine and a chance to contact other magicians your age. And it gets you into the headquarters in London. They do a show up there once a month."

A switch tripped in my head. A visit to London . . . a visit to London!! "Do you know if they've done this month's show yet?"

"I'm not sure, but we can check."

And I looked at Dad as he smiled at me and I remembered, just for a second, how close we used to be.

All that evening I kept thinking about going up to London. The idea curled round me. The Magic Circle was in Euston. I looked it up on the *A—Z* street map. Not close enough to Covent Garden, where Matt said he'd look for work. I'd ask Dad if we could do a detour and go there before we went to the show.

I had this hazed vision of bumping into him. I don't know how or why, but it would just happen. It had to. And as I thought about ways of meeting him, another idea drifted into the scene. People performed at Covent Garden. Clowns and musicians, body poppers and fire dancers. And magicians.

What if that was where it all suddenly happened for me? Maybe I wouldn't get as far as the Magic Circle. I would get discovered at Covent Garden. And what if, while the crowd were all roaring their approval, Matt came wandering over from his washing-up job to see what all the fuss was about (Dad had somehow been edited out of this fantasy).

Matt would see me. I wouldn't stop my act though. I'd carry on making rings float and bracelets disappear and everyone would be pressing round me saying things like, "Hey, look at this girl. She's incredible."

I'd catch Matt's eye and he'd wink and smile, and this time I wouldn't blush. At the end, when the crowd had drifted away, we'd hug and hold hands. Then we'd wander through the darkening streets while all the stars blinked and burned and somewhere nearby violins would play.

It wasn't a great area. Lots of tower blocks, most of them boarded up. I didn't feel that good about being there, to tell you the truth.

Danny led me along this alley that ran between two of the towers. It reeked of piss and booze and something else. I was starting to feel a bit of a nerd for just following Danny about. I mean he could have been anyone. Although every time he grinned it was hard to believe he was up to anything that wasn't okay.

We got to the end of the alley and it opened out round the back of the towers. There were pillars round that side, so you could get underneath the building. It must have been a car park once. I saw this fire burning, and a circle of chairs.

The chairs were all sorts. Armchairs. Office chairs. Even a settee. There were blokes in them, sitting drinking from cans and bottles. A few were talking but most were just slumped down staring at the flames. As the light flicked across them it made me think of Guy Fawkes. Blokes made of junk and old clothes and stuffed with newspaper.

We were standing among this mass of shacks, some under the tower block and some outside. The outside ones were dark huddles but I could pick out the ones near the fire. They looked pretty junky too—all bodged together with cardboard and plastic and planks of wood. This old biddy was hunched against a pillar, moving rubbish from one bin bag to another and muttering.

Danny led me towards the fire and I nearly fell over this bloke huddled asleep under a blanket. He moaned as I straightened up but he didn't move.

A skinny black-and-white dog limped towards me, barking and wagging her tail, and one of the blokes got up and came over to us. "Hush there, Bella. We're trying to ponder the mysteries of the universe. You're breaking into our thought flow." He was wearing these baggy pyjamas and a tartan dressing gown and I reckoned he looked pretty old but it was hard to be sure. He might just have lived a lot, if you get what I mean.

"Good evening, Danny." The pyjama bloke had a bottle of whisky in his hand. "Is your young friend seeking to sell us that pigeon?"

"This is Matt," Danny said. "He's a magician. Matt—meet the Professor."

The Professor shook my hand. "A pleasure to meet you, Magic Matt."

A skinny bloke who looked about my age wandered over, dragging on a joint. "We got roast pigeon tonight?" He had this white white skin and hollowed out eyes. I got this mad, sad idea that he was a sort of half ghost. Like he wasn't there yet, but he was going that way.

Danny was still talking. "Leave off, Spike. This is my mate Matt. He needs somewhere to doss."

Spike raised his eyebrows. "We're fully booked. No room at the inn."

"He's having my bash. I'm going to stay with Jen."

"Isn't she working?"

Danny shrugged. "She'll be finished by midnight." He sounded a bit down, but he took my elbow and led me towards one of the chairs. "Jen and me have got a kid together. Jordan. They're in a flat on the north side. You get housed if you've got a baby."

Spike slumped down in the nearest arm-chair and pulled a blanket up around him. "So maybe that's the answer. We should all have kids."

"Basic area of difficulty, my friend. You need a womb first." The Professor sat the other side of him and took a swig from his bottle.

"You need a womb to get a room." Spike coughed again.

I thought about the idea of everyone having kids just to get a place to live, and I didn't reckon it was a good way to come into the world. Though it probably wasn't any worse than being an "accident" with a nutter criminal dad who you'd never even known about.

Danny cracked open two cans of lager that were lined up round the edge of the fire and handed me one. I leant towards the flames, feeling the heat move through my hands. I was so cold. We'd walked a long way to get here, me and Danny.

I sipped the lager although I didn't really want it, and Bella crept forwards and rested her head on my knee. I stroked her ears, thinking about cavemen and wolves and how dogs first started being dogs, until a touch on my shoulder roused me and I turned round. This giant bloke was standing there holding a soggy slice of pizza right close to my face. "Want some?"

I shook my head. The lager was making me feel pretty vomity, to tell you the truth. "Not at the moment," I said, touching his arm as a way of showing him I appreciated the offer. "But thanks."

He frowned down at his arm, stared at me with these small puzzled eyes, then grunted and shuffled off.

"Shrewd move." Spike flicked the joint on the fire and picked up a can. "Tiny gets stuff from the bins."

"Maggots are an added speciality," said the Professor.

Spike did that coughing laugh again.

The fire burnt low. Danny drummed his fingers on the side of his chair. "What's the time?"

"Time you got a watch." More coughing. I could hear Spike breathe, like there was sandpaper in his chest or something.

Bella pressed closer to me. She was a sick dog. I could tell that just by touching her. I started to think about all the sick dogs in the world, and all the dossers huddled up under blankets, and all the starving giants living on maggoty pizzas. Just thinking about it got me so worn out and worn down that if Danny hadn't said, "Look, mate, I've got to go. It's a bit of a trek over to Jen's so I'll show you to your accommodation," I reckon I might have just sat there and cried.

My accommodation. It was right at the back. L-shaped. Made up of wood and poles and sheets of iron. A plastic curtain—the sort you put round showers—hung across the opening.

"It's great." I was whispering because I didn't know how many people might be dossing nearby.

"Not exactly the Ritz," Danny whispered back. "But go on in. It's not locked."

I ducked down and crawled past the shower curtain.

"It's pretty warm." I didn't know what else to say. And to tell you the truth, it was warm. Warmer than I'd been reckoning on. There were blankets and cushions and it wasn't that bad. I pushed my sports bag inside as far as it would go and settled Pox in it. Then I stuck my head back out. "How long you lived here?" Still whispering.

"About four years. Jen was in here with me until Jordan came. That's why it's a bit bigger than most."

I reckoned it was a long time, four years. In four years I'd be in my twenties. Grown-up. I couldn't get my head round that. "Will you be back tomorrow?"

"Sometime. Can't say when though, mate. Depends what slot I get at Covent Garden. Have a good kip."

"Cheers." I wanted to add "for everything" but I reckoned he might think I was a bit of a geek. And anyway, he was gone.

I peeled off my wet gear down to my boxers, and then pulled the blanket over me, right up to my chin. It was scratchy, but okay.

I closed my eyes and my head was spinning so I stayed still and kept my mouth shut. I couldn't puke in Danny's bash. It would be worse than puking in a real hotel. The curtain moved and cold air fell in, and then I felt Bella slink past and lie down next to me. I started stroking her and whispering and she whimpered a couple of times and wriggled so close she was almost on top of me, although I didn't mind. The voices started up but I was feeling so groggy I didn't really care if they were there or not.

Outside I heard the grunts of blokes talking. I could've been a kid listening to grown-ups at a party downstairs. Except for Spike's coughing. I never remembered hearing anyone cough that bad.

I didn't go to school the next day. It was the first time in my life I'd ever bunked off, but when I reached the gate I just couldn't go through.

Instead I turned round and retraced my steps until I reached the path that led to the castle. Looking up at the ruin I thought of words like desolate and gaunt. A jagged, ragged place.

It was slippy. The ground was ice hard and as I struggled up the hill the wind blasted into me. I pressed against it. The handrail over the bridge was still broken and I crossed carefully as a sting of hail slashed down, smattering the surface of the water. It had risen a lot in two weeks. I could just about make out the handle of the Tesco's trolley through the sludge.

I reached the shelter of the east wall and leant against it. Cold stone pressed through my jacket and I closed my eyes, listening to the rattle of rain. In the background the sea crashed and a squall of gulls screamed like lost souls. Bending down I picked up the grey rock I had "magicked" Matt's card under and held it against my cheek as if it would bring him closer, but it didn't. It felt distant. Indifferent.

I put the rock back down and my mind ran back to how Matt had looked to me that first day. Beautiful. Beautiful. There was more rubbish coming out of everyone's mouths than there was clogging up the moat. My mum and Matt's mum and Mr. Nelson and Pacey Macey and PC Barlow and Billy Owen. What was it like to have people on at you like that all the time?

A scatter of stones crumbled down from the top of one of the towers. I wondered where the pigeon was. And suddenly I decided I should be at home. Matt might have rung. He might be desperate to make contact.

I walked back along the bridge, gripping the wooden rail until I reached the part where it had split away. Glancing down I saw it drifting in the moat. And then I saw something else.

Muzzy under the surface, one end writhing softly with the movement of the water, was Matt's scarf. He must have dropped it. Either that, or someone like Billy Owen had dropped it for him.

I decided that I could rescue the scarf, take it home, and wash it. I'd get it ready to give back to Matt as a sort of gift. Crossing the bridge again, I started down the bank. Twice I nearly lost my grip. It would be easy to slip.

As soon as I was close enough I rolled my sleeve up and stretched forwards. My arm pushed elbow deep into the shock of cold. I grabbed the trailing end of Matt's scarf and tugged but it didn't move towards me. It seemed to be caught beneath the trolley. Crouching, I edged even nearer, winding the end so tightly that my wrist hurt. Then I pulled again. The trolley shifted, moving sideways. A dark shape began to rise. A splay of hair drifted and curled just below the skin of the water. It took a moment for me to understand. Then, with a hard, iced cry, I let the scarf slip away back into the reeds. The dark shape sank out of sight again.

It wasn't until I had stumbled back up the banks of the moat and reached the other side of the bridge that I started to scream.

It was morning. Still raining. I had this killer headache, my gut kept churning, and my tongue felt like it had grown fur or something.

Pox flapped up from the crook of my arm and stood on my chest. Bella stretched and yawned and thumped her tail.

When I opened the shower curtain to dump my wet gear outside, I got this shock. Tiny was sitting there, looking half drowned and like he'd been there all night. He rolled his sleeve up to show me something on his arm, but I didn't know what he was on about so I just grinned and nodded, and he seemed okay about that because he got up and lumbered off.

I went back inside and fumbled about, getting changed. The fresh gear was pretty crumpled but at least it was dry.

Someone coughed and I caught the whiff of cooking, and realised Spike was hunched down beside the fire. I went to join him, nodding at the old biddy who was still sorting through the bin bags, although she didn't nod back.

"Want a sausage?" Spike was turning them

in the flames with a rusty bit of wire. "Only we haven't got many. They won't hang about long once the others start foraging."

He caught a sausage with the wire and I took it from him. It was pretty black, but it tasted okay.

"There's bread under that plastic sheet. Sainsbury's delivered last night. Sleep all right?"

"Sort of. Do you always get stuff delivered by Sainsbury's?"

Spike gave me this look like he reckoned I had a few screws missing or something.

The Professor stumbled out to join us, rubbing his chin. "Morning, my friends." He was still in the dressing gown and pyjamas.

"Matt's been asking how often we place an order with Sainsbury's."

The Professor pulled a bag of sliced white from under the plastic and took the sausage Spike held out to him. "You've got a lot to learn, Magic Matt," he said. "But I would surmise that you're new to the game."

I didn't say anything but I felt pretty geeky, even though I didn't have a clue what "surmise" meant.

Spike coughed, and then said, "Super-markets bring us out-of-date stuff."

"Apart from the tipple." The Professor pulled a bottle from his dressing gown pocket. "To my lasting sorrow, it seems that good whisky doesn't go out of date." He unscrewed the lid and took a swig, then turned back to me. "Are you working today, my friend?"

"I don't work."

"He means busking," Spike told me. "Or whatever it is magicians do. Most blokes head out in the morning. Earn what they can. Come back in the evening." He glanced across at the huddled shape on the mattress. "Those that are up to it."

"Perform for us." The Professor took another swig and smiled at me. "Bring a little magic into our dreary lives."

I hesitated, remembering the way it had all gone so wrong at Happy Snacks, and then thought as long as I just stuck to one basic trick I'd be okay. And they were giving me bread and sausages and I reckoned I should give something back. I took that last twenty pence from out of my pocket, and fumbled with it on the inside of my jacket for a moment. They didn't notice the fumbling even though I was scared they would rumble me at any second.

"Shuffle this coin about behind your back,

choose a hand to keep it in, then close your fingers tight on both hands."

The Professor put his bottle down and took the twenty pence.

"Now stick your arms out in front of you."

He stretched his closed fists towards me and I narrowed my eyes, making it look like I was struggling to pick up his thought waves. Then I shook my head. "It's early in the morning to get this stuff coming through, but I've got a sense—I can't explain why—that it's in your left."

The Professor opened his fingers slowly and nodded round at Spike. "One out of one. A promising start."

I wanted to keep this edge of normality—like I was an ordinary bloke who could sometimes do something amazing. I reckoned that would be more convincing than just stunning them every second. So I shrugged. "Maybe I was lucky. Like I said, it's a bad time of day for vibes and stuff. Let's try it again." I noticed that the tips of his fingers were black and I was distracted for a moment. "You burned yourself?"

The Professor shook his head as he stuck his hands behind his back again. "Frostbite. Does that to you after years on the road. Don't look so shocked. Even the digits of a Magical Magician will prove to be vulnerable."

As I went back through the "struggling for thought waves" routine I remembered how cold I'd been, and reckoned I had to at least get some gloves. "Left."

The Professor opened his fingers. "Right second time. Or should I say left." He laughed but as he shuffled the coin again his eyes had this new respect in them. "Ready."

I looked from hand to hand, making out things were flowing more easily now. "You're a stubborn git. You haven't moved it. It's still in your left."

"Now I *am* impressed. Three out of three is pushing at the edges of coincidence. Let's see if you can run to four."

"Left again."

Spike gave a low whistle as the Professor opened his fingers.

I went for a fifth.

They were both sort of gaping at me.

"I can't do any more." I shook my head, like I was suddenly drained. "My brain's aching." It was too. I had a stinking hangover and anyway I reckoned I should cut while I was on top—

before either of them worked out what I was up to.

"Intriguing, my friend." The Professor handed me back my twenty pence. "Maybe you'll teach me the secret some time."

I shrugged. "I don't know the secret. It just happens. I can't always get it right." I was getting into the whole act idea, and I understood what Erin had meant about getting people to believe in you. I'd pulled off two decent tricks in two days. Not bad for a beginner.

Spike shoved another sausage under my nose and as I took it I was suddenly pretty up about everything. Even the vomity hangover feeling faded a bit. I sat in a chair, my head sorting through plans of what I was going to do next, although nothing seemed too urgent. It was like there was time for everything.

"The Army's here," a voice called from somewhere outside the pillars.

That jolted me. I nearly choked on the sausage and jumped up thinking we were all about to be gunned down or something. Then this woman with a cap saying "Salvation Army" appeared dragging a green bag.

"New boots and shoes," she called, tipping the contents onto the floor.

This stream of blokes came out of the shelters, yanking off their old boots and swapping them for new. Although they weren't exactly new, of course. Just newer. It smelt a bit rank, to tell you the truth.

I thought for a second about trying some myself but I thought I might get the other dossers' backs up. It wasn't like I really belonged there or anything. I might have been a bit more pushy if she'd brought gloves.

This time they made me go to the police station. There was a room with a video camera.

PC Barlow sat opposite me across a table. "You've had a rough time, and I wouldn't have got you here unless it was important. I hope you can appreciate that we need to follow this through as quickly as we can. Once this interview is over your dad will be free to take you back home again."

I glanced at Dad, who was sitting in the corner of the interview room, and he smiled at me. I tried to smile back but my lips wouldn't stretch that way. I could still see that dark shape. It rose in my head again and again. It would rise like that forever.

I realised PC Barlow was talking. "Why were you so keen to get hold of Matthew's scarf?"

Matt's scarf. Round Kirsty's neck. I didn't understand it, but I could see how it must look to the police. I had to protect Matt. I had to be careful. "I just thought he'd want it back."

"It can't have been pleasant though. The bank was wet and slippery. You might easily have slipped in yourself."

I tightened my lips and shrugged.

PC Barlow rubbed his chin with his hand. "You say you and Matthew were good friends."

"Yes."

"Nothing more?"

"Nothing more." Careful. Careful.

I was sorry about Kirsty. Devastated about Kirsty. But I knew Matt hadn't hurt her. He couldn't hurt a fly. I wasn't going to say things that they might twist the wrong way. The dark shape kept rising and I felt tired and sick and wished I could go home.

PC Barlow put a small plastic bag down on the table. "Going back to the magic you told me about yesterday—do you recognise this?"

It was mottled and creased, but I'd have known that card even if it had spent a million years buried under rock. The two of hearts.

I like you. Lots.

Had Matt left it beside his bed? Or under his pillow?

I rubbed my arms with my hands. "Did you get that from Matt's mum?"

"Kirsty had it. It was in her pocket, in the back of her purse." He slid it across the table to me. "Without taking it out of the bag, would you say this is Matthew's writing?"

"It's . . . it's mine."

"And the card?"

"That's mine too."

"And were you aware that you'd lost it?"

"I . . . I gave it away. To Matt."

PC Barlow leaned forwards, as if something in his brain had started ticking.

"Why?" Tick. Tick. Tick.

What game was this? What tricks did PC Barlow have up his sleeve? "I give cards away sometimes. It's part of my act."

I like you. Lots.

Tick. Tick. Tick.

"It's a special thing, a message like this. Something that you would have thought Matt would want to treasure." He kept his eyes on me. "I wonder how Kirsty got hold of it?"

I looked down at the card, trying to cut away from his stare. How *had* she got it? Why was it in her purse? A picture came into my mind that I didn't want to see. "I don't know."

PC Barlow shook his head as if he was grappling with questions that would explain the meaning of life. There was a weight of silence between us.

Tick tick tick.

Only this time it wasn't PC Barlow who was ticking. It was me.

I went off with Spike. Pretty well everyone was going somewhere. You get this idea that homeless people doss about all day, but this lot didn't. Or at least, they all got up and went off to doss about somewhere else. Most of them anyway. The Professor and the huddled blanket bloke didn't look like they were going anywhere.

"I busk at Leicester Square." Spike pulled one of those penny whistle things out of his pocket. "It's not rich pickings. Not like Covent Garden. But you can do all right this time of year."

Pox was up on my shoulder and Bella trotted a few paces behind. She wasn't limping now, and she didn't seem quite so sick. In fact she was bouncing about like a puppy, to tell you the truth. I tried to shoo her away because I didn't reckon she'd have a great time busking, but she just sat down and looked at me like she'd made up her mind and she didn't give a stuff what I thought about it.

"Do you ever get trouble? You know—people roughing you up?"

Spike headed down the steps into the blokes' bogs. "Not in the daytime. You get a bit of abuse. Usually posh gits who think you're out there because you're too lazy to get a job. Like it's an easy option. Nighttime's different. I've been knocked about at night before. It's best not to sleep too deeply if you're on the streets at night."

He started to peel off his clothes and ran the hot tap, splashing it all over himself. He was still coughing like he was coughing for England. I joined him with the hot water. I couldn't go about stinking if he wasn't. We even washed our feet, hoicking them up over the edge of the basin. We left puddles of dirt on the floor when we'd done.

Spike had a toothbrush and when he offered it to me I didn't say no, but I hoped I'd at least make enough dosh to buy one for myself. That and some gloves. I scrubbed my teeth while Pox perched at the edge of the basin and splatted droppings all over the side. I had to clean it off with the edge of my sleeve.

We went back out up the steps to where Bella was waiting and pressed on towards Leicester Square. Loads of people passed us.

"Spare any change, mate. Spare any change, mate."

Nobody stopped.

"We should split now," Spike said, when we got to the square. "We won't be good for each other if we're together. We won't look vulnerable enough. But if you need me, I'll be at the entrance to the subway. Unless I get moved on."

I nodded, standing like a nerd as he walked away.

A few minutes later I could hear this tinny version of "I saw Mummy kissing Santa Claus." That, and the coughing.

I didn't know what the hell to do. I got Erin's cards from out of my pocket and flicked through them a few times. "Pick a card. Any card. Pick a card. Any card." I sounded pretty geeky. I was pretty geeky. It was one thing to do stuff close up, with people like Annie and the Professor already watching. It was something else again trying to pull it off out here. I couldn't even say it loud enough to be heard.

I remembered a time in the school playground when I'd got this set of Robo War cards. I didn't have a clue what Robo War was, but everyone had them and they were swapping them and so I collected enough to join in. Except whatever cards I had, no one seemed to want them. I waved them about a few times but in the end I stuffed them back in my pocket. I stopped bothering with them after that.

I wondered whether to do that now? Stop, I mean. Except I needed dosh—I was still thinking about those gloves and that toothbrush.

There was this nail on the pavement and I picked it up, showing it to this bloke who was walking by. He jumped back like he reckoned I was going to try and pick his nose with it or something, which at least made a couple of other people turn and look. With a bit of jacket groping that was slightly less fumbly than I'd been earlier with Spike and the Professor, I managed to get the nail to float. I guess it looked more impressive than cards because a few more people glanced back and smiled, although they may have been more interested in Bella and Pox. Nobody stopped though.

And then I remembered something else I used to do in the school playground. Something that *had* got a decent reaction. I've got these wrists that are sort of flexible. I can twist them about and from a certain angle it looks like they're rotating. I never like doing it because it always hurts like hell but at least it gets people looking. I crouched, putting my palm flat on the pavement, and began.

"Here's a quid to make sure you stop doing that," someone called. He chucked a coin at me. It hit the ground and spun off out of my reach.

A different voice. American. "Oh, stop it. It's so gross. You can hear the bone click." Fifty pence that time.

I kept going.

"That's disgusting." Ten pence more.

Someone else dropped a penny. A foreign coin rolled towards me.

I reckoned I'd have to remove my whole arm or something to make enough.

This copper came over. "I don't quite know what you're doing, but firstly it's illegal. And secondly it's insane. If you don't want to spend the night in a prison hospital for those of unsound mind, I suggest you move on."

I straightened slowly, rubbing my arm. It was pretty sore, to tell you the truth.

"Street performance is forbidden in this area. What's your name?"

That shook me. He might know my face or something. Mum might have put posters out on me. I rubbed my arm again, then squared up to his gaze. It took a minute to get up the guts, but I had to do something to get him off my back—so I leant forwards and took a twenty pence piece from behind his ear.

"Hey—did you see that?" A couple of blokes started laughing and one pressed a quid into my hand.

A woman pulled a fiver from out of her purse.

The copper pulled his mobile from out of his belt.

"What the hell you doing?" Spike was suddenly right beside me, grabbing my arm.

"I'm just . . ."

He dragged me away. "Leg it, mate. You don't want that sort of publicity. That copper was just about to pull you in."

We ran for it, but with Spike's wheezing and my stitch we were pretty useless so we gave up. The copper wasn't following us anyway. I reckoned we couldn't have been much of a catch for him, which must have meant the country wasn't riddled with posters and messages from Mum begging me to come home. Why should she? She'd got rid of her criminal nutter accident son. I pushed the thoughts of her from my head and thought about the fiver and the coins I'd left behind on the pavement. I'd made a quid, but that wouldn't even stretch to a toothbrush. So I stuck my other twenty with the new pound coin and Spike and me got some coffee instead. He hadn't earned a bean.

I stared out of my window towards the castle. PC Barlow had let me come home. I'd been a mess anyway. I hadn't been telling him anything that made sense. It seemed as if I'd been given a giant jigsaw puzzle from a jumble sale and half the pieces were missing. There were bits of blue sky—the first day we'd met; the evenings spent showing him magic in my kitchen; that sizzling snog.

And there were cloudy bits too—those questions about fancying someone; Kirsty wearing his scarf; I like you. Lots.

I played with the pieces. Frowned over them. Fussed with them. I tried to remember every conversation we'd ever had. Every moment we'd spent together. I shuffled through the memories of that first meeting. Would Matt have come round to my house if I hadn't asked him? Had he really wanted to learn magic? Had he even really liked me? Uncertainty spread like something rotting.

Another memory shifted in the sludge. "You wouldn't want to stick your hand in that. You'd probably pull a body out or something."

The moment floated up as if weeds had suddenly parted. And suddenly all the missing bits turned up under the lid. I was so stupid. Stupid stupid stupid.

It was Kirsty that he'd fancied.

I like you. Lots.

How could I have imagined it would have been anything else? Had he shown her my tricks? Told her my secrets? What if they'd been together on the bridge? He'd gone too far. She'd pushed him away. What if . . .

I sank my head into my hands. This was hard. So hard. Beautiful. Beautiful.

"He's a liability." Spike was still wheezing like an old dog. "He was doing magic on a copper, for God's sake."

"You've got to learn the rules, mate. The rules of the street." Danny took his arm from round Jen's shoulder, and she lifted a squalling Jordan out from his pram.

Spike went on and on, telling everyone round that fire about the twenty pence and the copper. You'd have thought I'd brought a stash of heroin out from under his helmet, the way they all started shaking their heads. I'm not that keen on hanging around listening while people have a go at me, so I walked off. I got my sports bag from Danny's bash and just left.

Danny caught me up as I turned into the street. "Hang on, mate," he said. "We're trying to look out for you. I swear we are."

I wasn't going to listen. Pox was on my shoulder

and Bella was by my side and I reckoned I'd just keep walking. One foot and then another. One foot and then another.

"Look behind you," said Danny. "They don't want you to go."

I turned. Hanging around watching from the end of the alley were Spike, the Professor, and Tiny.

"You've got something special, mate. Think of what's been happening."

"What d'you mean?"

"That bonkers woman yesterday. The copper this morning. The Professor's been going on and on about that coin thing. And Tiny's convinced you cured his eczema just by touching his arm."

"That's crap. I didn't even know he had eczema."

"Doesn't matter, mate. The point is, for whatever reason, people are starting to believe in you. And that goes for me too. I think you're different. And I like you."

I just sort of stared at him then. After a minute he went sort of swimmy and out of focus and it was because I was crying, which was a pretty naff thing to do. But I couldn't help it. No one had ever said stuff like that to me before. I pressed my eyelids with the back of my hand. "Okay." I gave him this sniffy sort of grin. "I'll stay."

I'd been stupid. Stupid. And I wanted to hurt him. It must be true that love is close to hate, because I hated him then. I really really hated him. And it wasn't so much because of what he must have done to Kirsty. It was because of what he'd done to me.

The camcorder was on my dressing table, with that film still in it—that film when he'd talked about the body in the moat. It wasn't much, but it was all I had. My hands shook as I picked it up. I put it down again. I picked it up. I put it down.

Then suddenly I went downstairs to where Mum was ironing in the kitchen. "I need to talk to PC Barlow again." I gripped the camcorder, holding it in front of me as if it was a gun. "I've got something that might be important."

Within two hours I was back in the interview room with PC Barlow. Mum was in the corner, a police tape recorder was running, and Matt's face began to move into focus on the screen.

PC Barlow pulled his chair close to mine.

"I'll turn it off any time you want, but it might jog your memory. There might be something new you remember."

My memory pulled out things I didn't want. His eyes. His voice. The way his hair kinked in the rain.

The film ran on. ". . . It's got bad stuff round it. You wouldn't want to put your hand in that. You might pull a body out or something . . ."

PC Barlow ran it again.

And again.

You might pull a body out . . . You might pull a body out . . . You might pull a body out . . .

And each time the odd panicked look in Matt's eyes made me shivering cold. He must have planned it. He must have known.

PC Barlow stopped the film. "Is there anything else? However small. However insignificant."

I pushed the question through my head. Nothing came. Nothing. Only Matt with Kirsty and Kirsty with Matt and just in that moment I wished he was at the bottom of the moat too. Or at least in prison. I wanted him locked away forever.

PC Barlow turned off the video player. "So can we go back through that last meeting? The conversation by the bridge."

"It wasn't much. We weren't there long. He'd just rung me and said that he needed to see me . . ."

"No reason why?"

"No. He just sounded . . . upset."

"And what did he say?"

"He was going away. Everything was wrong and . . ." I stopped for a moment, staring at PC Barlow. "There was something about an accident."

PC Barlow leaned forwards in his chair, and I knew everything would hang on whatever I said next. And when the idea came it didn't seem such a terrible thing to do. It was only a nudge on from what Matt had really said. It was nearly true—so close to being true. I was hardly changing anything. "Matt said—'What I did to her was an accident.'"

My head slumped forwards and I closed my eyes. I could hear the soft whirr of the police tape recorder running. It caught my silence as impartially as it had caught my words.

"That's a vital piece of information, Erin. Why didn't you tell us before?"

"I . . . I didn't want it to be true."

"And would you be prepared to repeat that in court?"

I looked at my hands, watching tears bleed down onto them. "Yes."

And one part of me thought that PC Barlow with his huge ticking brain would know what I'd done. His alarm would go off. He wouldn't let me do this.

But he just kept staring. "Thank you, Erin. You've made a good decision. This statement may make all the difference. Now, knowing Matt as well as you do, where do you think he might have gone . . . ?"

A good decision. All the difference. One tiny twist to the truth.

The old biddy had just finished sorting through some more rubbish bags when Danny swivelled his chair round and poked me in the ribs. "I'm bored, mate—magic me something."

I stopped watching the old biddy and stared up into the sky like I was waiting for all the energy of the universe to tune into me. Then I got Erin's carved box and key from out of my jacket pocket, and handed them to him. "There's three dials here. Set a number on each of them. I'll turn away so I can't see what you're doing." I swivelled my chair round so I was facing the opposite direction.

"Okay, mate. Done that."

"Now lock the box up with that key."

"Done that."

I swivelled back to face him. "Now run the numbers through your mind."

"Okay. Doing that, too."

"Make them bigger. Brighter. Make them like they're really glowing."

I reckon my voice sounded pretty good. I was keeping it soft, like I was dark and mysterious. I wished I could have tried out that voice on Kirsty. I stared into Danny's eyes. He stared back. I put on this frown to make it look as though the number was coming through and I was trying to see it properly. I noticed Danny had these green eyes with gold flecks, and I remembered hearing someone say once that the eyes mirrored the soul. I reckoned, as I kept frowning, that Danny's soul must be pretty okay.

Suddenly he put the box down under his chair, leaned forwards, and punched me in the chest. All the mystery stuff got jolted away and just for a second I reckoned I'd been a right sucker and he was going to do me in.

Only then I saw he was laughing. Doubled-up laughing. "Oh Christ, mate. I'm sorry. I couldn't keep a straight face. I was never that good at those staring games."

And then the naffness of the whole thing got me laughing too. We slid down out of the swivel chairs and rolled onto the ground. I was laughing so hard my side hurt worse than when I'd had that killer stitch. Danny punched me again and I punched him back. We wrestled like a couple of kids in the playground and a stack of that old biddy's bags toppled and fell on us. All this rubbish spewed out and we were both still creasing up like it was the funniest thing that had ever happened. And to tell you the truth, for me it was. I'd never laughed like that in my life. I'd never felt that good. Never. Not even close. And then the old biddy came over and started muttering and picking up the rubbish again.

"Sorry, Kathie," said Danny. "We'll give you a hand."

"Yeah, sorry," I said. And as we brushed what muck we could off ourselves and stood up to help her I turned to Danny and said, "Four hundred and fifty-seven!"

He dropped the scrunched-up old newspaper he was holding and took a step back like he wanted to get a better view. "Christ, mate. That *was* the number. You got it right. You've got to do something with all this magic. You could blow everyone away if it takes off."

Back at home I sat in the front room while Mum went to ring Dad. I had a blanket round me and I picked at the edges, rolling the fluff into tiny tufts. I hurt. I ached. Matt's face filled my head. I hadn't known anything about him. He was just an illusion. A trick of the mind.

Everyone else knew how it was done, but not me. Stupid. Stupid. Stupid.

I heard the door open and a moment later felt an arm round my shoulder. "Are you okay?"

I let myself lean into Dad. "I can't believe I didn't know what he was like." Stupid. Stupid. Stupid.

"People like that can be very . . . charming."

People like that.

People like Matt.

"What will happen to him now?"

"I don't know." Dad squeezed me. "But you've told the police as much as you can. They've got an idea of where they might find him, and you've given them evidence of something that sounds pretty close to a confession."

I wanted to tell Dad what I'd done. I wanted to hear him say that tiny twists of the truth were okay, if the end justified the means. It was what I was trying to believe.

"I'm not sure if I should have said so much. I'm not sure if . . ."

"Sweetheart—you didn't have a choice. You couldn't have let him keep roaming the streets. He'd do it again. People like that always do."

People like that.

People like Matt.

Dad was right. PC Barlow was right. What I'd done was right. And it wasn't as if I'd said I'd seen Matt dragging a screaming Kirsty down to the moat and pushing her in. I'd hardly said anything. Just the tiniest, tiniest twist.

Dad squeezed me tighter. "And whatever happens, we *will* get through it. I promise."

I noticed the "we" and I noticed that I didn't mind.

*

Danny opened the can of lager he'd bought with his day's fire juggling dosh, and passed it to me. I swigged a bit even though I still wasn't that keen on the taste, then handed it back. There were a few scraps of out-of-date bread in the Sainsbury's bag and I took a slice out, holding it towards the fire on a piece of bent wire, the way Spike had done with the sausages.

When it smelt right I gave it to Danny.

"Jen has had an idea," said Danny, crunching into the toast, then glancing over to where Jen was curled in the armchair feeding Jordan. "Tell him, Jen."

I found it hard to look across at her. She was breastfeeding and even though it was dark the firelight still lit up glimpses of white flesh that I wasn't used to seeing. I listened to the rain smack into the mud nearby and started on the next slice of bread. "What's that?"

"You should go with Danny tomorrow. To Covent Garden." She sounded like she really cared and I felt this rush of warmth for her even though I couldn't look at her.

"Get a slot there," she went on. "Do your magic act at a decent place and get some decent dosh for it."

I gave her the next piece of toast, sort of staring at her left ear while I handed it over. "I haven't got an act. Just bits of stuff that this girl was showing me back at Leigh Cove. I haven't been learning it long."

"Christ, mate." Danny sounded like he wanted to stuff my head into one of Kathie's bin bags. "You just about blew me away with that four hundred and fifty-seven thing. Give yourself a break."

"We'll get a gang together." Jen paused while she switched Jordan from one side to the other and I kept my eyes fixed back on the fire. "You start to put on a show—we'll just act it. The gang will do anything you say. If you tell them they're thinking of four hundred and fifty-seven, they'll say yes. If you tell them they grew up in the North Pole, they'll say yes. If you tell them they're all aliens from outer space, they'll say yes. They'll back you up. Trust us."

"Why would they do that? Why would strangers act out stuff like that for me?" We were the only ones still up and there was still a manky bit of crust left so I reckoned that must be mine.

"I've already told you, mate—we look out for each other. And after tomorrow, if you don't make a packet, we'll never get you to do it again."

I didn't say anything. I was still thinking it through.

"And we'll be mates whatever. Trust us on that, too."

I still didn't reckon I could pull it off. Not with a proper real-life audience. I was still pretty fumbly. But then Spike and the Professor and Danny had all gone for my tricks. And Annie. Especially Annie.

I broke the bread and gave bits to Pox and Bella, then crammed the rest into my mouth without bothering to toast it. I was pretty hungry, to tell you the truth. I started thinking about the gloves and the toothbrush. I thought about the dosh I owed Mum. I thought about maybe buying a train ticket and going back to explain things to Kirsty sometime.

"Go through it with me now then," I said. "I'll tell you the sort of stuff I can do."

I got up early. I hadn't slept, but I had made a new plan.

"NEW WAYS AND NEW DAYS."

I would forget about Matt. I'd just have the magic from now on. I'd create an act—not just that of a scraggy schoolgirl going round doing things out of the blue, but I'd work on having an aura of mystery. I'd live the part. Maybe get a black cat and wild hair and keep stuffed doves in my room. Forget *Gossip* and that whole thing of having to be like everyone else. I would be myself. Bigger than myself. Enigmatic and magical and mysterious. And I'd get myself known. Famous. I'd be on stage. On telly. In films. People would queue for days just to see me.

Magic would save me. It always had and it always would.

I flicked through a deck of cards and dropped them suddenly. I tried to make the white dove fly but the feathers fell away, exposing a mash of wire and old rags.

Outside it was raining again.

"We're first," said Danny, as we stood outside the transport museum.

A waiter from the café next door was setting tables out under an awning, and we went across and sat down. Danny ordered coffee.

"Hiya." This girl stuck her violin case against the wall and called over. "It's fr-fr-fr-freezing this morning."

I stared at her—sort of gawped as she wandered over. Sarah!

"Haven't you remembered your long johns?" Danny grinned.

"I'm wearing two pairs." She giggled. "But it's still not enough. I can't stop sh-sh-sh-shivering. I picked up this hand warmer from a camping shop too. I can't hold the bow if my hands ice up." She pulled a tin box from her pocket and pressed her fingers against it.

"So how come you're here?" asked Danny. "Aren't you going home for Christmas?"

"I will do, but I'm trying to put it off for as long as I can. You know what it's like, going home. And the money I get here helps the grant to stretch. You never know—if I have a good morning I might even get you a Christmas pressie." She smiled at him, and then her eyes flicked over to me. "Hey—I remember that pigeon. You're the magician by the river."

My face must have gone this gawky puce. I'd told her I reckoned performing was a way of life. She'd expect me to be at least half decent when I did my bit.

Sarah picked up Danny's coffee and sipped it. "Disgusting. No sugar." Then she turned back to me. "Have you busked here before?"

"First time." I felt vomity just saying it.

She smiled at me, like she knew I'd made up all that performer stuff, and she didn't mind.

"The street is your stage. Draw an invisible circle on those cobbles, and keep the audience on the other side of it. You just do it by where you walk. Where you stand. It's called 'the edge.' You need to know where your edge is."

It was getting busier. There were more places opening and more people about. The vomity feeling got worse. Bella pressed herself against my leg and Pox shifted on my left shoulder.

"Street performance is the purest form of entertainment." Sarah dropped three cubes of sugar into Danny's coffee and stirred it slowly. "Think about it. If people are inside a building and they've bought a ticket, they'll stay even if you're crap. If you can hold people's attention on the street, when it's cold or it's wet and they don't have to watch you, then you've really got something."

I didn't feel that great, hearing her say that. What if I didn't have "something"? What if I didn't have anything?

But I still kept sitting there, because, to tell you the truth, just being there felt okay. More than okay. I wasn't the geek walking by trying to think of some amazing witty thing that might give me an excuse to keep me hanging round her. *She* was talking to me. They all were. I was part of the gang.

And that was why, an hour later, when Danny said, "Right, mate. Let's give it a go," I checked that Erin's stuff was all in the right places and got up.

Danny made this sweeping bow as if he was in front of the whole of the Royal Opera House or something, although the sky was blacking over and there weren't many people watching. Spike was there, and even though it was ice cold I reckoned he'd lost that "washed-out ghost" look. Jen was there too, with Jordan. A second later I spotted the Professor. He looked even older, and his jacket was too small and his trousers were too long, but he was dressed, and it got me that he'd gone to all that trouble. The rest of them I didn't know. They didn't look like dossers, but then why should they? Jen and Danny probably knew a stack of people from all sorts of places.

Danny grinned his toothless grin at everyone. "Okay, ladies and gentlemen, this is Matt the Magician. Matt the Mind-Reader. Matt the Maker of Miracles."

★

Downstairs in the hall the phone went. Two minutes later Mum knocked on my door.

"That was PC Barlow." She came over and put her arm round me. "Just to let us know that they've got someone covering Covent Garden."

Once, when I was at infant school, I was a shepherd in the school play. I was wearing this dressing gown with a tea towel over my head and I was supposed to say, "Look yonder, a new star is rising."

Only one of the kings had dropped his jar of frankincense and I was so caught up pointing yonder at the back of the hall that I fell over it. It wasn't a big falling over and I got up pretty quick but by the time I'd started pointing yonder again this twinkly music had begun and the angels came dancing on. They sort of shuffled me to the side of the stage and I never got to say anything at all.

Mum pretended it was okay but she went into this tidying-up frenzy when we got home and she wouldn't look at me. I wasn't keen on doing shows and stuff after that.

"Welcome, everybody." Danny was talking in this real "roll-up, roll-up" sort of voice. "Magic Matt is going to start with coins. He'll tell a member of this audience which hand they are holding a coin in—just by tuning into their thought waves."

This bloke with dreadlocks and nose rings stepped forwards. "Hey," he said, nodding at me, "I'm up for that."

"Okay." I tried to do the mystery voice but laryngitis frog-throat came out instead. "Get a coin and shuffle it behind your back. Move it from hand to hand and then hold your arms out in front of you."

Dreadlocks Nose Rings took a quid from his pocket and did as I said and we ran through it three times.

"Three right out of three. Truly bizarre. Do you do lottery numbers?" Dreadlocks Nose Rings clapped me on the shoulder and dropped the quid in this box that Danny had stuck near "the edge." I felt loads better, like Jen and Danny's mates really were going to look out for me.

Bella padded over and sniffed the box like she hoped Dreadlocks Nose Rings might have dropped food in it, but she didn't seem bothered that he hadn't. She just came back and pressed herself against my leg again.

"And now Magic Matt's going to do more amazing magic."

There was a stack of people gathering. I caught the eye of this girl who was all done up like she was off for an interview or something. "Have you got anything sharp? Those tweezer things that girls use? Or small scissors?"

She dug in her handbag and pulled out a nail file.

"That'll do." I took it from her and stared at the sky. Then I looked round slowly at the audience, and this time the mystery voice worked okay. "I need complete silence. If this goes wrong, it hurts."

I held the file horizontally between my palms and pulled my hands away slowly. The file floated in the air.

Nobody spoke, but I could sense this amazement coming off them and it gave me a real high, to tell you the truth. Like I really was someone. I frowned to show how hard I was concentrating and started to bring my hands in towards the file, only I kept closing until the tips of it pressed through my palms and out through the backs of my hands. There was this sort of group shudder and I froze the moment just for effect, then slowly opened my hands again. The file dropped away and I held my palms outwards for everyone to see.

"No blood." I grinned.

I gave the girl back her file and she kept turning it over and over. "I don't get it. I *really* don't get it. How did you *do* that? How did you do that?" She was half laughing and half crying and people pressed closer. I was feeling pretty good by then, like I'd definitely cracked it. It crossed my mind that I should call Erin later. I had to thank her because she'd given me all this.

And then I saw a woman come barging through all the others. She was pushing this wheelchair with a Father Christmas balloon tied to the handle, and the balloon was bouncing about getting chucked around as it knocked against everyone.

My gut shrank. Annie. I could tell that any second she would start having a go at me, and if I legged it this time there was a good chance the whole lot of them would come hurtling after me. I'd never get away. So I reckoned the best thing to do would be to talk to Annie. Or at least to the kid. I crouched down in front of the wheelchair. Ella stared over my left shoulder where Pox was still perched. She had that blanked-out look again. I felt crashing down sad for her, and for Annie, and for her dad with those eyes that I reckoned would never stop streaming whether he was chopping onions or not.

I put my hand out to hold hers and started whispering that I was sorry for the way the world had turned out for her, even though I knew she couldn't hear. Only as I touched her I started to feel weird—like everything was distant and I was hanging between time again. My hands burnt hot and the voices seemed sort of urgent like they were telling me to listen— listen properly—and not push them away.

Ella's hand moved under mine. It wasn't much, but I could tell she was trying to get a grip on my fingers. I gripped her back and I reckoned my hands would be on fire any minute, but I couldn't stop. Something was happening. Something was really happening.

And then I felt this touch on my shoulder.

All of that weird stuff just crashed away and I stood up in a daze to find Dreadlocks Nose Rings standing there staring at me. I couldn't think what the hell he was doing but I got this feeling like there was bad stuff round him and I lifted my hands in the air and started to say, "Hey, mate—what's wrong?" only he flipped this wallet thing open to show me his identity card and said, "Are you Matthew Mason?"

"Yes."

"I'm DC Blaine from Charing Cross police station. I'm arresting you on suspicion of the murder of Kirsty Carter."

As we drove to the inquest I told myself I hoped I wouldn't see him. I wrote his name on a piece of paper and then screwed it up, tearing it into tiny pieces.

"You okay, sweetheart?" Dad's eyes met mine in the rear-view mirror.

"Fine." I wound down the window and hurled the scraps of paper into the frost-white morning.

"All this is just a formality." PC Barlow came over as we walked in. "We've got sufficient evidence. Unfortunately, because the body was found in water there's no foolproof DNA samples and forensics found nothing relevant on the clothes Matthew was picked up in. But your film, together with your statement, backs up the case. We should have enough to nail him."

He touched my shoulder. For the rest of that morning I felt the weight where his hand had been.

The coroner was squat and toady, sifting through a file and croaking out questions about Matt. About me. About that last afternoon.

"Did you notice anything unusual about Matthew Mason during that final meeting by the bridge?"

In my mind I wrote Matt's name. In my mind I tore it up. "I could see he was upset. I thought it was because he was going away."

"So he seemed distressed? Agitated?"

"Yes."

"I gather from your statement that it was a stormy day. Are you certain you could hear his words clearly against the wind?"

This was a chance. I could still straighten that twisted lie.

I hesitated. Matt with Kirsty. Kirsty with Matt.

I like you. Lots.

"Yes."

"I'm sorry—could you repeat that?"

Write his name. Tear it up. Write his name. Tear it up. I looked into the toad eyes. "Yes."

"Thank you." The coroner closed the file with a snap and turned to the jury. "We'll now study details of the pathologist's report . . ."

"I want to go," I whispered to Dad. "I don't feel well."

Dad held me, gripping my elbow as we left.

And it was then that I saw him. I hadn't expected him to be there. PC Barlow had said Matt wouldn't have to go to the inquest—the inquest was only to establish the cause of death. It wasn't like the trial because that was set for later. It was being held at the Crown Court on April 17. Matt saw me too. Looked straight at me. He seemed hollowed out. Shrunken. And it burnt through me that I couldn't imagine him doing it. Couldn't imagine him hurting anybody ever.

Stupid stupid stupid.

When I got home I wrote his name with a giant marker pen. And this time I didn't just tear it up. This time I stabbed it to shreds with the broken wire from the dove.

Danny visited today. He does that a lot, and I reckon it's pretty good of him. The weather's better now because it's nearly Easter, but hitching up here must be a slog. He's my main visitor—him and Mum, and I have a better time with him. Mum just brings me homemade oatcakes and cries a lot. She reckons I did it, although she never says. She probably thinks it's because I had a nutter criminal dad. Like I was destined to end up this way or something.

"How's Pox?" I said. We were facing each other across a table, and Danny glanced at the warder behind me. He has to sit there, just to make sure I don't do a Houdini and escape inside Danny's trouser leg or something.

"Pox is doing great, mate. Spike has knocked up a shelter for her and she shares it with Bella. She's part of the scene."

"You should use her in your fire act. She's pretty tame and she'll get you noticed."

Danny shook his head. "She's saving herself for you. Bella too. That dog's not sick like she used to be, but she's been drooping around like a wet weekend since you've been gone."

I didn't answer, but I reckoned they'd both have a long wait.

"And Sarah . . ." Danny leaned forwards in his chair. ". . . she came and saw me at Covent Garden yesterday. She's got some mates who are studying law, and they've told her the evidence against you is wobbly. They say that film can't prove anything on its own. The only hard facts the police have got are the scarf, and Erin's word. If just one of those two got taken out of the story, the whole plot would collapse."

"Leave it," I said. "It's best if I don't think like that." I didn't get why Sarah was bothering, to tell you the truth. She hardly knew me. And then Erin, who I'd reckoned was my mate, had done the opposite. It still gutted me, the stuff she'd pulled out. Danny reckoned she must have had a thing for me and then got hacked off about something, but there'd been nothing like that going on between us. I just didn't get it.

Through the high window on the wall opposite I could see that the sun was setting. Spilling gold.

I turned back to Danny. "I still can't get over Kirsty," I said. "Her being gone and everything." The voices keep whispering that I could have stopped it. They reckon they'd sent that black shape that I'd seen hurtling down on her as a sign. They go on about how much they could help me if I let them. They're getting pretty bossy, to tell you the truth. I listen because I have to. There's no loud music here to drown them out, and the humming doesn't work any-more. I talk to them sometimes, although I don't say anything out loud. I'm stupid, but I'm not stupid.

"I'm sorry, mate." Danny looked like he wanted to make everything all right but couldn't think what the hell to say.

"It's okay." We both went quiet again.

To tell you the truth, I'm getting used to the idea of being in here. I've done a few tricks—just the really basic stuff because I can hardly stitch nail files into my cuffs in this place—and they really went for it even though I reckon I'm still pretty slow. Yesterday this bloke Wayne Webb, who's got a scar stretching halfway across his skull, was pretty keen to learn the one where you make someone's watch show up in their back pocket; but it's only the wardens who wear watches here and I'm not going to take risks like that. And anyway he doesn't want to learn magic. He wants to learn a better way to nick watches.

The first time I saw Wayne Webb I wondered if he was my dad. I do that a lot in here—wonder if prisoners are my nutter criminal dad. Although I don't stare at them while I'm thinking about it or anything. It's not a good idea to stare at other prisoners. Especially those with scars stretching halfway across their skulls.

"So—just three days to go then, mate." I could hear Danny struggling to keep his voice sounding okay.

I tried to keep my voice okay too. "And it's all pretty well settled, whatever Sarah's mates say."

There is a way out. My solicitor reckons I could plead guilty and make out that I'm not right in the head, but I won't go for it. I'd rather get banged up than give people a chance to think more stuff like that about me.

"Sarah likes you, mate," Danny said suddenly. "I mean *likes* you."

"Has she told you?" I felt knocked out hearing him say that. And crashing down sad, too. I wanted to start punching the table I was so hacked off. What a waste. What a waste.

"She's always talking about you. And she thinks you've got a gift. Not just your act, but something bigger. Something you might not even know about."

"What d'you mean?"

"You never saw it—but that kid that day—her mum really lost it after you left. She started crying and saying that the kid was smiling and she hadn't smiled in years and the whole thing was a miracle."

"That was just Annie. She's bonkers."

"Except she comes back sometimes, bringing the kid with her. She always asks questions about you. I haven't told her where you are because she'd probably turn up outside with a placard and it might not go down that well, but the kid looks fine. Chats to me and everything."

"You never told me."

"I was like you at first. I thought the woman was bonkers. But after Sarah said that 'gift' stuff, I started wondering. I mean—supposing you have got something bigger, mate? Supposing you could mix magic with real miracles. You'd be the new sensation. Crowds would follow you through the streets. Think what you could do—what you could be."

For a second I got a picture in my head, like he might be on to something. Like it could really happen. And then I got the crashing down in my gut feeling again, because it didn't matter if I was the weirdest weirdo in the world or some amazing miracle maker, I was going to go down anyway. It wouldn't make any difference.

"Time to go." The warden came over to Danny.

"Take it easy, mate." Danny touched my arm. "And don't give up."

I didn't answer. Because I already had.

Mum comes into my room. "How are you feeling about Friday?"

I stop practising the trick where a card someone has chosen actually begins to glow from inside the deck, and watch my lips open and shut. "Okay." Every time I practise in the mirror I see someone I don't recognise. Or like. And it's nothing to do with the wild spiky hair or the mysterious magician image.

I try the trick again. I saw it done when I was on holiday once, only the magician pretended it was a "healing" card. He claimed that touching the glowing card could cure all sorts of problems. Everyone was impressed and he made loads of money, but I walked away. That sort of magic doesn't exist. I wish it did, but only people like doctors and nurses can really heal you.

Lily and Lucy appear, crawling in after Warlock. He shoots under my bed, his black kitten tail fluffed out in panic.

"It'll be over after that." Mum stops Lucy from climbing up Dotty's pole and hoists her onto her hip. "You won't have to think about Matt again. You can draw a line under that whole terrible time."

I don't answer, but she is wrong. Every day he is the first thing I think about when I wake up. And I have never learnt to live with that tiny twist to the truth.

I lie down on the floor to practise a new levitation idea. I have to twist suddenly and do a sort of press up, keeping my body parallel to the floor and lifting one leg so that it's stretched and straight. Dad has rigged up a mechanical device that drops a sheet over me, and to an audience it will look as if my body is rising slowly.

Mum watches for a moment. "Is Tom coming round tonight?"

I sit up again and shrug. I know what she is trying to do. She is trying to make me go out with Tom as a way of getting over Matt.

It won't work. I can't pull feelings out of a hat; but at least we're friends.

"IT'S GREAT TO BE MATES."

"He's coming over to make a video of me running through my audition routine. I want to see what this levitating looks like from all angles."

I smile at Mum, and she smiles back. I am doing all the things I said I'd do. New acts. New hair. And I've even got the cat. But I can't feel the buzz of magic anymore. I am a mechanical mask person.

From under the bed there is the sound of paper being shredded and Mum frowns. "Your kitten's demolishing something."

"It's just those *Gossip* magazines. I was going to bring them down for his litter tray anyway."

"BE BRAVE, BE BOLD—CHUCK OUT WHAT'S OLD."

Lily begins to climb on my head. I get hold of her and tickle her. She laughs and screeches as if being tickled is the most wonderful thing in the world.

Downstairs, the phone rings. "That'll be Dad." Mum grabs Lily just seconds before Warlock springs back out and attacks her toes. "He's coming round later. He said he'd ring first to see if we all wanted fish and chips. I'll get him to bring some for Tom, shall I?"

"Okay." I nod as she gathers up the twins, then turns and goes.

It is Dad who has sorted out the Magic Circle audition. Dad who bought me Warlock. Things aren't brilliant between us, but he's trying. And I'm not any better than him now. That tiny twist to the truth. I've stopped needing Dad to be perfect.

I pick Warlock up and go to the window. The sun is sinking behind the castle walls, soaking the sky with gold. Beautiful. Beautiful.

I've never been back. Never even been along Station Road since Matt got arrested. I always trek the long way round to school.

Matt is pleading not guilty. I felt sick when I heard that. I thought he'd admit it once he got picked up. The police are pinning their case on to the scarf, and the "confession."

Across the road a stone-white pigeon lands by the gutter and scratches around the drain. I remember Matt's pigeon. The way it